Kill Alone

Kill Series – Book Three

Richard A. Powell II

ISBN: 978-0-578-50927-3

www.richardapowellii.com

Other works by Richard A. Powell II:

Kill Team: Kill Series – Book Two (2018)
Kill Academy: Kill Series - Book One (2017)
RejectGuy99 (2015)
A Room Full of Keys (2013)
Neither Snow, Nor Rain, Nor Zombie
Infection & Other Strange Tales (2012)

Available by order at bookstores and online
worldwide

ACKNOWLEDGEMENTS

Thanks again Darrel and Amy for reading my work and helping me get it ready to present to the world. And to all the people who keep reading – I thank you most of all.

Part I
My Past

1

There's a woman looking back at me from the mirror. I recognize her but she's not the same person I once knew. For safety's sake, she's now blonde, although, it's still just past shoulder-length. She's wearing a navy-blue dress and flats. To complete the ensemble, she's sporting wire-framed glasses despite having near perfect vision. Through those fake lenses it's easy to see the eyes of a tired woman, a heartbroken woman, one who appears closer to thirty-five years old than her actual age of twenty-five. The last two years have worn her down more than the previous ten combined.

To get the information I need about my past, the best option is to appear more mature. My new look is stark and somewhat befuddling. I can't remember the last time I put on a dress and some fancy shoes, and now that I've got them on, I know why I avoid them. I prefer the freedom of movement that comes with a good ol' pair of blue jeans, a well-worn hoodie, and some sneakers. Plus, my lifestyle is better suited for gear that will make it easier to run like hell or blend into a crowd of people when needed.

It's only been ten days since I walked away from the Kill Team house, from Ollie, from AWT, from my life as a paid assassin. My team was decimated. Turned out we never had a chance. Vick may never walk again having been literally and figuratively stabbed in the back by Emily. I've been told I put Emily down, and somewhere in my heart I know I did. Problem is, my mind won't let me go there anymore, at least not in my visual memory.

Putting aside the massive clusterfuck of a mission in Texas and Ollie's lack of honesty, the time has arrived for me to go deeper into my past than my position at AWT would ever allow. I have to listen to my gut on this, and my gut has been telling me to go solo for a while. The company will hunt me, relentlessly, I know that. If my training has been worth anything, it will be in its ability to keep me hidden, alive, and on track to the truth.

Just south of Hampton Township, north of Pittsburgh, Pennsylvania, I found a little German themed bed and breakfast with three rooms upstairs and one bigger suite on the third floor. I chose the latter. Something about the higher vantage point makes me feel more secure. I planted four wireless cameras around the house, just in case. If anyone starts snooping around, I'll hopefully see them coming.

This place comes with a stern but hospitable German woman, Greta, as innkeeper, complete with a demand to come down for a freshly prepared breakfast of schnitzel, hard fried eggs, extra crunchy toast, and scalloped potatoes with enough vinegar to curl your nose hairs. It's all delicious and a wonderful change of pace from my usual over-sized coffee.

Today, I'm all gussied up to go visit the business office of Allister Coal, hopefully to uncover some information about my parents. I have their names. Daniel and Anzu Jones. She went by Annie. According to a few news reports I was able to uncover on the internet, they disappeared twenty years ago without a trace. They had a five-year-old daughter who was also never seen again. The three of them up and vanished like smoke in the wind. The daughter, me, is alive and mostly well. It's been a rough twenty years but I'm hanging in there. In my current state of affairs, that may be fleeting. My parents appear to have fallen victim to the bad end of a murder-for-hire contract through the very company I have, up until recently, been trained and employed by. I suppose that's another reason why I felt compelled to leave. How could I, in good conscience, continue to work at AWT without knowing the full details of my parent's end and how I coincidently wound up serving the responsible company?

After eating my full German breakfast and sucking down two cups of coffee, I went on my way north on Route 8. About twenty minutes later, I took a left on Baker's Hill Road and went another twenty minutes.

I'm arriving at the Allister Coal business office at 9:45 am. The building looks to be about two thousand square feet, single story, beige vinyl siding, green metal roof. The parking lot is gravel with thirteen cars. There's a large gated fence to the left leading to another parking lot and the entrance to the mine itself.

I back into a space, ten from the front door, and leave my rust bucket to go in. The temp is chilly for late September, so I had to pick up a nice, tan trench coat yesterday to go with my fancy dress outfit. With how I look right now, I doubt anyone I know would recognize me. I have my faux blonde hair pulled up into a tortoise shell colored clip and proceed to do my best impression of Dina as I walk through the front door.

Upon entering the tiled foyer, I see a tiny waiting room to the right with three green chairs and two oak tables between them. Magazines are scattered about. There's a gold cart in the corner with a k-cup machine and all the necessary accoutrements. The wall to my left is covered with small picture frames and a bulletin board. A distinct smell of charcoal and glass cleaner fills the air.

Straight ahead sits a reception desk complete with the obligatory fifty-something receptionist, older desktop computer, and flashing office phone.

I step forward and smile.

"How can I help you?" the receptionist asks with some surprise, no doubt from having an unannounced guest. Hard to believe anyone would just wander into such a remote place.

"Hello. I'm Samantha Wentworth." I answer with as much charm as I can gather. "This is probably going to sound a little weird, but I represent a law firm in Baltimore that is trying to track down some information about a couple that worked here some twenty years ago. There are some estate issues we're trying to clear up."

"Oh? Is that right? Twenty years is a long time ago."

"It most definitely is. I'm sorry, I didn't catch your name."

"Cathy. I'm the office manager ... and part time receptionist when needed."

"Pleasure to meet you."

She nods and smiles. "So, exactly what kind of information are you looking for?"

"Nothing too complicated. My client is attempting to track down any heirs that might be due part of a wealthy estate. Our client had no children, so we're digging around the extended family to see if there is anyone left."

"I see. And what were the names of the employees you mentioned?"

"Daniel and Anzu Jones."

Her eyes light up. "Of course. I remember them well. Terrible they never figured out what to happened to them, or little Kiki. Kyoko was their daughter's name, but everyone called her Kiki. Greatest mystery these parts have ever known."

I put my hand over my mouth in an attempt to hide my emotions. I'm pretty sure my jaw would have dropped to the floor had I not. It's taking everything in my being not to run out of the building and burst into tears. I turn around and fake a cough, staying there for a few moments to gather myself. When I turn back with watery eyes, I find an outstretched arm holding a tissue. I take it. "Thank you. You wouldn't happen to have glass of water or a vending machine? Got a little something caught in my throat."

"I'll be right back. Grab you a bottle of water."

She leaves her chair and disappears through a door to her left. She returns in less than thirty seconds with a local store brand eight-ounce bottle of water.

"Here you are, hun."

"Thank you so much." I take the bottle, twist the cap off, and drink a third of it. "Oh boy. That's better. Thanks again."

"You're welcome. So, the Jones family, I assume you know their story, being with a law firm, I'm sure you've done some digging."

"Some, yes. So, you knew them, personally?"

"I did. I hired Annie myself. She did accounting here. Daniel was a supervisor for some of the miners, though he mostly worked up here in the office. You mentioned something about heirs earlier. As far as I know, they had no family around here, never even mentioned any, not to me anyway."

"Hmmm, that's interesting. Well, I'm looking for anybody, even distant, distant relatives. Maybe I could talk to their neighbors. You wouldn't happen to remember where they lived? I know it was a long time ago."

"Sure, I remember. Been there two dozen times, at least. It was a little farm house out on County Road 145, north edge of Hampton. Don't think anybody lives there now."

"That's great. You've helped me more than you know. I have one more request, and ... this may be more than you're willing to give up, confidentiality and all, but you wouldn't happen to have any paper records on Daniel and Annie, paystubs, employment records, copy of their driver's licenses, things like that? No big deal if it's asking too much or been too long."

"Well," Cathy pauses, puzzling over the ask. She looks me square in the eyes, trying to find a reason to refuse. "It's been a long time and I'm pretty sure they ain't coming back. What harm could there be? I tell you what, give me a minute to go back and find their files and make a few copies. I doubt there'll be much, but you can have whatever there is." She points in the direction of the bulletin board wall. "You see that black frame, second from the left on the top row? Grab it and I'll be right back."

I turn with nervous hesitation to the wall and spot the frame Cathy referred to. I take a few steps forward and fix eyes on the color photo of a man and woman standing side by side, a little girl standing in front of them.

I pull the frame off the wall and take a closer look. I don't think I've ever seen myself in a picture prior to eight or nine years old. So innocent. And my parents. Their faces have always been a blur, featureless, unknown. Now, here they are, smiling and believing they have a lifetime worth of memories ahead of them. Damn it. I can't help but notice how much I look like Annie. I have her eyes and cheekbones. To keep my shit together, I flip the frame over and decide to deal with it later.

I go back to the desk and wait for Cathy. She returns with two green file folders and a manila envelope. She places the folders on the desk in front of her and hands the envelope to me. "I hope these help. It's all we had. I see you found the photo." She extends her hand. I offer up the photo. She stares at it and smiles. "That was taken at the Pioneer Days Festival in Pittsburgh. I don't remember the year. Mid-nineties. Shame no one ever figured out what happened to them. They were a nice family." Cathy looks to me, then looks back down to the photo, then back to me again. She's working it out.

I need to bolt. Hopefully the blonde hair is enough to throw her off.

"Here." She hands the photo back to me. "Keep it. Might be of use to ya in your search for answers." Her tone tells me I've been discovered. Shit. "Say, if you ever figure out what happened, I'd sure be curious to know." She smiles.

"I'll tell you what, if I discover anything and I'm ever back this way, I'll swing over and buy you lunch."

She nods and sits down.

"Could be something, could be nothing, but as a favor, should anyone come around asking about someone matching my description, I was never here." I give her a big wink.

"This never happened."

I spin around and walk to the exit. Turning back, I say, "Thank you again."

"My pleasure ... Kiki."

I leave without acknowledging her words or looking back.

In the car, I place the frame and the envelope on the passenger seat and drive away with a stomach and mind full of mixed emotions. I need time to process, but unfortunately, I don't have any to give. If I stick around this area too long, I'll be in danger, and I just hope Cathy's revelation doesn't put her life in danger either.

A few moments later back in the business office of Allister Coal...

From a door behind Cathy, a man emerges, stepping to right behind her chair.

"Hey, who was that? the man asks.

"Hey, Bill. No one. Somebody asking for directions."

"Oh." Bill glances down to the folders on Cathy's desk, his eyes wandering right to the tab in the upper right-hand corner. Written in blue ink, it read: Jones, Daniel. His expression sours. As he turns to leave, he spots something unusual about the bulletin board wall. A frame is missing. He knows exactly which photo it was. He rushes out of the room without saying another word. He has a phone call to make.

2

The morning after Josey went AWOL...

The halls and offices in the academy part of AWT were quiet. There was no new class of recruits to be trained, no veterans wandering the halls. Ollie was suspended for two weeks and could be anywhere in the world. Dina had left that very morning for an already planned trip to Jacksonville, Florida to visit family. That left Li Xia sitting in her office, pondering the future of AWT, and subsequently, her own fate.

Like mornings on most days, Li Xia sat behind her desk listening to the BBC News on her computer while reading through the daily or weekly reports from department heads. The only thing on her plate that day was further analysis of the Texas Kill Team contract in an attempt to find any hole that might exist in their procedures, preparation, or personnel. She had been at the company many years and they had never once been infiltrated by a third party, let alone through the puppetry of an existing team member.

She couldn't help but conclude that the company-wide blind spot had been possible because of the inner turmoil revolving around Madame K and Josey Baldwin. *Wouldn't it just be easier to boot Josey? Certainly, Madame K herself can see the root breaking through the foundation of their house. Why not cut the damn tree down instead of blowing up the building? Makes no sense.*

The cell phone sitting on her desk came to life with a ring, pulling Li Xia from her thoughts. She looked to the screen. It was the Kill Team House security line. She picked up the phone and swiped.

"What?"

"Ma'am, we may have a problem," the man answered, his hesitation clear.

"What now?" Li Xia questioned with reluctance at hearing the answer. "Go on. Spit it out."

"Josey Baldwin is gone."

Li Xia didn't immediately answer. She took in one large, deep breath through her nose like the big, bad wolf about to blow down some little piggy's house, then she exhaled.

Enough time went by that the man on the line began to worry.

"Ma'am, you still there?"

"Yes, I'm here. When was the last time anyone saw her?"

"Log shows her coming in yesterday. No one has seen her since."

"Damn it! Were you idiots not told to monitor her, closely?"

"Yes, ma'am. There is no excuse. We have no idea how she left without detection."

"I have my ideas. She could be to Texas or Montana by now. Just keep a close eye out in case she returns, though I doubt she will. You call me the second you hear or see anything."

"Yes, ma'am."

She ended the call and dreaded the one she would need to make. *Then again,* she thought, *this might require an in-person office visit.* With no Dina or Ollie though, she'd bear the entire wrath of Madame K, and that, she dreaded most of all.

Li Xia stood before Madame K after revealing the fact

Josey had run away again. There was a silence that went beyond comfortable and into the realm of unnerving. The entire time, Madame K had her left hand around her ceramic tea mug like she was ready to pick it up for a drink but her hand never moved.

Taking a chance at Madame K not being ready to advance the conversation, Li Xia spoke, "I'm sure you can imagine the state Josey might be in, considering the Texas debacle. She may just be blowing off steam. But then again. What would you like us to do?"

"Simple. I want her found and brought in ... alive. Use every resource."

"Ok."

"There's a war coming," Madame K said.

"I'd say the war is already here."

"And, which side will you be defending?"

"I'm a company woman."

"Well, very soon, this company may look quite a bit different."

Li Xia shrugged her shoulders, revealing nothing.

"Always the cryptic neutral."

"Can I be forthright?"

"I would hope you always are."

"And still wake up tomorrow?"

"That's harsh. You're one of my most trusted advisors."

"Now, who's not being forthright?"

"I'm boring of this. Speak your mind. No retaliation."

"You're grip on this company is slipping. You know it, everyone knows it. I don't see a way to fix it short of you leaving. I don't think that's necessarily a bad thing. Times change, people change. Certainly, you didn't think you'd do this forever. It's a miracle all of us have lasted this long."

Madame K's body language said nothing to Li Xia, in fact, her hand was still on the mug, but behind the eyes, Li Xia could swear there were actually flames growing.

"Interesting. Your free pass has expired. Go deal with Josey. I want updates the second there are any. You're dismissed."

Li Xia took a few steps back before turning, finally taking a breath, and leaving the office.

With no facial expression, all the tension in Madame K's body manifested itself into her left hand. A few seconds later, the mug shattered in her palm, splashing tea on the desk. A small trail of blood ran side by side with the remnants of the Earl Grey.

3

I find the house rather quickly. It rests in the middle of a two-mile long stretch of country road. There are several other houses in this mile, on both sides of the street, all separated by at least an acre or two. The land is a combination of heavily treed patches, pasture land, tiny free-flowing creeks, and several landowner's attempts to keep every piece of scrap metal, junker car, and old tire in the county. On first sight, it's hard to tell how many of the homes are still occupied, except for the one I used to call home. Half the windows are shattered and there's a piece of plywood nailed over the space that once had the front door.

I pull my car into the barely discernable driveway, made now of mostly weeds and very little gravel. I decide the time has come for me to change into something less lawyer and more stalker. I reach around to the backseat and grab a neatly folded and stacked outfit. With some twisting, snaking, and damn near popping my arm out of the socket, I manage to get the lawyer outfit off and the blue jeans, black long-sleeved shirt, burgundy zip-up hoodie, and black work boots on. I keep the one pistol strapped under my left arm, over the shirt, and I have a small gun on my right ankle.

Upon leaving the vehicle, I jog the thirty feet back down

to the road and check in both directions for traffic. It's quiet. Can't be too careful. In the nearly two weeks since my escape, I have yet to come across any AWT lackeys, but it's only a matter of time before they will track me down, especially if I keep hanging around high profile locations.

I walk back toward the house, and like a surge of electricity has hit the back of my brain, a vision, or maybe a memory floats through my head. I see the house before me, cleaner and somehow larger. At my feet, the driveway is weed-free and covered in pearly white gravel. I turn and watch a large yellow school bus drive away before continuing on to the house.

I open my eyes and once again see the dilapidated house. My current reality doesn't last long. In a flash, the previous memory fades and another replaces it.

I hear the familiar squeak of metal on metal. Laughter. To my left not far from a giant red oak tree is a two-person swing set. A girl is sitting on one of the red plastic planks, flying back and forth through the air. I can feel the breeze cooling my face on a paltry summer day, just as she must have. A girl's voice, my voice, keeps saying *faster Daddy, higher Daddy*.

Suddenly, I'm back to the present. I glance to the left and find the now broken down and rusted swing set still near that giant oak tree. The right side has collapsed to the ground. Neither seat is still attached.

There are emotions running through me, ones I can't ever remember experiencing. Childhood nostalgia? Parental love? They overwhelm me. I take a step to my right and use my hand to brace myself on the mirror of my car to keep from crumbling to the ground under weak knees. I lose my breath for a moment. My lower lip quivers. I close my eyes and try to gather myself. My mind races with the possibilities of a once happy and normal life, now lost to tragedy and pain. The joy turns to anger as I open my eyes and bear witness to a house left in the past and the family that once lived there. My family.

Almost everything in my being is telling me to run away, but seeing as how this will likely be the one and only time I ever get to see the house, I'm feeling compelled to find a way in. I'm sure there were other people that lived here after we did, so it's not like I'm going to find any family heirlooms or a lost doll or anything, but the sheer sight of it may trigger more long forgotten memories, perhaps even some insight into my final days here. It seems I'm stuck in a big pile of *what if* right now and I only want to dig deeper.

Without a few power tools, there's no getting in the front doorway, but I think the window to the left of that is low enough and missing enough glass that I should be able to crawl through. I walk over to the window, pulling my gun from its sheath. I use the butt to clear out any remaining pieces of glass still attached to the pane. I turn around and take another look across the property and the road. The area is quiet, so I holster my weapon and crawl through. After sliding across the threshold, I tumble to the floor beneath the window. Luckily, there is no furniture to break my fall, just musty carpet. I hop to my feet, dust the crap off my pants and hoodie, and survey the room before me.

I cover my mouth and nose. "Christ, this place stinks." I can't spend much time in here as the smell is overwhelming. There's a combination of wet dog, mold and mildew, and compost. I breathe in too much of this shit, I'm going to end up in the emergency room.

Trying hard not to think about the odor, I take careful steps through the living room to a dining room with adjacent kitchen at the back of the house. There are no real furnishings to speak of - a broken wooden chair, an old duffle bag. The floor is littered mostly with chunks of plaster wall, broken glass, and pieces of the ceiling that had fallen down after taking on too much water from the leaky roof. The single-story house is tiny with only two bedrooms and a bath, and a crawlspace instead of a basement.

I get no instant recognition of this place, no feelings of being home, nothing. Perhaps there is nothing left on the inside as familiar as the exterior.

Not a memory, but a thought crosses my mind about my parents and how they may have died. If they were indeed taken out by an assassin, did they die here, in the house? Did they suffer? Where was I when this whole thing went down?

They could have been snatched from anywhere, but if I were the one doing the recon and Point on that assignment, I can't imagine a more perfect location to do the job. Isolated. Remote. Low traffic. Check. Check. Check.

I'm disgusted by the fact I can so easily equate my current skills and training to what might have happened to my parents. In this moment, I hate AWT, I hate Madame K, but most of all, I hate myself for what I've become.

Tired of being too near to this misery, I flee the house and return to my car, unsure where or who to turn to next. I settle back into the driver's seat and take a moment to relax, clear my mind. Despite his lying ass keeping a big secret from me, a talk with Ollie might calm me down. I haven't stopped thinking about it for days. He revealed to me that he knew all along about the contract against my parents. He didn't believe there was anything fishy going on with me being recruited to the same company that happened to be the one that killed my parents and ruined my life, unbeknownst to me, of course, until now. With some time to think about it, I do believe him, but I'm still mad as hell about it. Shit. Who else can I count on right now if not Ollie?

Amatto, maybe? He appears to be on my side, but when push comes to shove, I have a feeling he'll look out for himself. Who wouldn't? I do get the impression that he's more loyal to Ollie than Madame K, which favors me.

The Dean? She's pretty much been World War II Switzerland in all this. Every question I try to ask her has ended up in some riddle or metaphorical sidestepping. I can't really blame her. In this business, death is often the result of misguided alliances.

And then there's Dina. Admittedly, I don't care much for her part in all this. I understand it. I can even appreciate it to some degree, but I just hate having someone smarter than me inside my head. On the plus side, she has been aligned with Ollie on most things, and that bodes well for me.

My train of thought is broken by the sound of a vehicle pulling into the drive behind me. My eyes go to the rearview mirror and I see an early 90s full-size pickup truck. Not the first choice I would imagine from someone at AWT looking to take me out, but then again, look at the crap I'm driving.

I pull the gun from under my arm, pop the safety, and exit the vehicle after placing the gun inside the front pouch of my hoodie. I leave my hand on it.

I stay near my car, door open, in case I need to duck behind it for cover. The man inside the truck is older, maybe in his early sixties or perhaps a youthful seventy. I lessen my guard. Pretty sure we're not looking at an AWT assassin here. He opens the door of his truck and hops out. He throws up a quick wave, friendly, then starts to walk toward me.

When he gets close, I smile and give a wave back.

"You lost or something, sweetheart?" the old man asks, more concern than chafe in his voice. He's clean shaven, mostly bald with a little thin gray hair just above the ears. His jeans are faded gray and he's wearing a casual dark purple, long-sleeved button-up sport shirt. He looks like a guy who is enjoying his retirement, but not too much.

"Nope. Just taking a stroll down memory lane. I had family that used to live here ... long time ago. You live nearby?"

"I do. Two properties down that way." He points east. "Ain't no one lived here in quite some time. Can't say I recognize you. I'm Gary Bowden. I manage some of the farm properties around here. And you are?"

I struggle for a moment in telling him who I am. I start to say Josey Baldwin but I choke on the words. Probably safer for him if he doesn't hear that name.

"Amanda Jones. Did you know the people who used to live here, like twenty years ago, Daniel and Annie Jones?"

"Daniel and Annie Jones? I sure did. Craziest damn thing

I ever heard of, their disappearance. Vanished off the face of the Earth. Hadn't thought about it in years. There ever any resolution in all that?"

I shake my head.

"Real sorry to hear that, miss. Damn shame. I remember them being good people. Funny, rambunctious little kid too. Always asking questions. Had to know everything. Ummm ... little Kiki, right?"

"Yeah. My, uh ... cousin."

"You look a little like her."

"I've heard that. If I could ask, is there anything interesting you remember about them, a funny story or something? I was so young when they disappeared. I barely remember them anymore."

"Well, let me think." He rubs his jaw line with his right hand as he tries to recall. He puts up his index finger. "Oh yes, I had almost forgotten. I remember little Kiki; she might have been three years old. She had wandered away from the house one day and no one could find her. Annie was in a damn panic, running around all over the place looking for her. In a matter of minutes, she had the police to the house, neighbors scouring the area, including myself and my late wife, Liza. I guess Liza was out near the property line behind our house when she heard giggling and tiny yelps.

"She started yelling for me, so I went running back there. When I got to this little culvert, I found Liza sitting on the ground, and right in front her was little Kiki and four or five puppies that couldn't have been more than three to four weeks old. There was no sign of the momma dog.

"Apparently, little Kiki heard the pups crying from all the way over at her house and she just followed the sound. Got everyone up in a frenzy that day, but it turned out okay in the end. She'd probably be a veterinarian today, if ... well, ya know."

I smile as a tear falls from my left eye. I wipe away the moisture.

Gary reaches around and gives me a one-armed hug.

"Didn't mean to upset you."

"No, no. Bittersweet tears. Thank you for that. Made my day."

"You're most welcome. So, you find what you were looking for out here?"

"More than I expected." As I the say the words, a late model black sedan drives by, slowing a bit at first, then speeds off. It got my spidey-sense all tingling. "Well, I really do gotta get going. Thank you again." I reach out and offer a hand.

He extends his own hand and we shake. "Pleasure to meet you, Amanda. Come down for a coffee if you're ever 'round this area again."

"I will. Thank you. So long." We exchange waves.

I get in my car and quickly start it. I pull around his truck as he's still getting in and position myself between him and the road to shield him in case that sedan circles back. I look in both directions but don't see anyone. I wait for Gary to turn his truck around and pull up behind me before I take off. I have a strong feeling that I've lingered too long around here. The heat is rising. Time to bolt. I'll make a fast trip to the B and B to gather my things, but then I'm on the road again. To where, I'm not entirely sure yet.

4

I'm on high alert as I pull away from the bed and breakfast. I sat on the bed after packing up and had a good, sobbing like a little baby kind of cry. With my limited memories emerging, the story from Gary, and my inability to stop looking at the photo from Cathy, twenty years of emotional turmoil, longing, and regret spilled out like a broken dam. Once I got myself together, I hit the road and drove south into West Virginia without once looking back or stopping.

When the fear of being followed subsides, I pull off the road at a gas station in a remote town I've never heard of so I can go to the bathroom, get a drink and some grub, pump gas, and make a call. Over the last few days, I've softened on Ollie. With my world coming down around me, I feel like I need an ally.

I bring up Ollie's number on the dummy phone and press SEND.

"It's me."

"Hey."

We speak over each other for a moment.

"Sorry," Ollie says.

"No, no, you go ahead."

"I just wanted to say, I'm sorry this is happening to you. You didn't ask for any of this."

"Well, I appreciate that, Ollie."

"Are you safe? Spot any goons?"

"Possibly one today. I'm all clear for the moment. Say, how is Vick?"

"He's doing okay. Still can't walk but he's working with Greg. Kind of his academy apprentice now. He seems to like it."

"That's great."

"Gives him something to do. He was crawling out of his skin just laying in a bed all day. We're working with a doctor in Germany on some cutting-edge spinal stimulation using stem cells, so he has some hope I guess."

"I'm happy to hear that. So, as far as my AWOL situation, what's the order from the top?"

"No idea. Still suspended. If I had to guess, I'd say it's a bring you in ... alive, for now. If it goes on too long, who knows. Got a plan or figure anything out?"

"Got some family info but nothing useful, more sentimental. Without being able to travel back in time, or Madame K just flat out telling us what happened, I don't see any other options."

"Hmmm. You might be on to something there."

"In what way? You want to help me kidnap and torture Madame K? Bleed all the information out of her. Let's do it!"

"In your dreams. Even at her age, she'd tear us both apart."

"She can't be all that."

"If we had Amatto and The Dean with us, maybe. She's the original, the mold in which all of us were formed. She wrote the fuckin' book. Got it? Don't you dare even think about confronting her."

"I got it, I got it. So, what's your idea?"

"Let me make a phone call and I'll get back to you in a few minutes. Okay?"

"Fine."

"Okay. Call you back in a minute."

The call ends. I'm left to wonder. I inhale half a bag of beef jerky and a diet cola while I wait.

I constantly scan my surroundings, searching for that one out of place vehicle or some city slicker that looks like he turned down the wrong road. After that asshole in Texas snuck up on me and put a knife to my throat, I swore I'd never let that happen again.

I decide to get back on the road and use a Bluetooth earpiece to answer Ollie's return call. I don't even know where I'm going, just heading south and east on the interstate.

After ten more minutes, my phone finally rings.

"Hey," I answer.

"So, I'm not sure how you're going to feel about this idea, but just listen and keep an open mind."

"Ummm ... okay."

"I just talked to Dina."

"Oh, here we go."

"Open ... mind."

"Okay, okay. Go ahead."

"You mentioned earlier about traveling back in time and there might be a way we can sort of do that. I'm sure you've heard of hypnosis?"

"Yeeeeeah. Why?"

"I remember talking to Dina once about using hypnosis to undercover repressed memories in trauma patients. She said that it can be effective if the patient is open to it. This could be a tool for us to utilize here."

"Sounds like some serious hocus pocus bullshit."

"Generally, I would agree with you on that. However, I trust Dina as much as I do anyone, and she's probably smarter than you and I combined. If she says it can help, I believe her."

I sigh loud enough to make sure Ollie can hear me.

"We've hit a wall here, Josey. I think this might be our best shot at getting something."

I hate to admit it, but he's probably right, assuming it will work. I'm a skeptic and a pessimist. I generally equate hypnosis with Sylvia Browne, Astrology, and Ouija boards. I'll be hard-pressed to completely buy in.

"So, how will this work then, if ... and it's a big if, if I say yes?"

"Simple. You'd meet with Dina. She performs the hypnosis. That's it."

"Oh yeah, super simple. You do realize I'm on the run from AWT, the place she's still employed at, and I'm sure being watched like a hawk. Simple."

"Well, she just happens to be on vacation in Florida, and I don't think Madame K has any reason to expect the two of you would be in cahoots. You'd have to be careful, of course, but I think it's doable."

"And she's actually down with this?"

"She's as curious as we are to uncover the truth. But just remember, she's not like us. She may work for AWT, but she couldn't do what we do. Her risk in helping us is much greater."

"All the more reason not to get her involved."

"She understands the risk and is willing to help. All you have to do is get down to Jacksonville. Can you get there in a day or two?"

"I could. I just don't know if I want to."

"Unless you have some other bright idea, I'd say do it, or come back in to AWT and let's try to work this whole situation out with Madame K. She's dangerous but not always unreasonable."

"That ain't happening. I need to know the truth about how and why I came to be with Rosemary, and who pulled the trigger on my parents."

"And when you get that information, what then?"

"A reckoning."

"Josey, this is not going to end the way you want it to."

"It will end the way it ends."

"I can see there's no steering you away here, so just go to

Dina."

"Okay. Send me the Florida deets. I'll contact you again afterwards."

"Be extra ... fuckin' ... careful."

"I will. Thanks, Ollie. I couldn't do this without you."

"Don't make me regret it."

"I'll do my best. Bye."

"Okay. Bye."

5

I drove for a while before stopping outside of Athens, Georgia. I convinced a cute guy behind the desk at a nice hotel to let me stay there with no credit card, no id, cash only. He even snuck me some room service after I promised him a hundred-dollar tip. I think he was hoping for some action up in my room, but I'm just not into scrawny little nineteen-year old's. Sorry kid. Not that I'm much older than he is, but somehow, I feel older. I'm certainly more worn and I've sure as hell seem some shit, shit that would curl him into a fetal position and make him cry for his momma.

I woke up today and finished the drive to Jacksonville. After our session, I intend to dump my car and get another one to take me to my next unknown destination.

For security purposes, we've agreed to meet at an IHOP during the busy lunch rush. I'm already here scouting out the place, checking for blind spots, exits, any vulnerabilities. The parking lot is easy. It's only on two sides of the building, so from the booth I'm sitting in, I can see the main door, the primary lot entrance and exit, and both sides of the parking lot. With all the patrons, there is no way someone would make a move on us while we're here. Survey us, yes. Take us out, no.

I'm sipping on shitty coffee that needs extra creamer to make it palatable when a strange woman comes in the restaurant and walks straight toward me. I casually place my right hand inside my unzipped hoodie and rest in on the gun strapped under my arm. As the woman gets closer, I'm taken aback when her face comes into focus. Up to this point, I've ever only seen Dina in formal business clothes, so when she hits the table wearing a casual, black long-sleeved tunic and blue jeans, I need a double-take to verify what I'm seeing.

"You seem confused," Dina says after arriving at the table. "I bet it's a little disconcerting to see me outside of the office. May I sit?"

"Please." I wave her into the booth. "And yeah, I've never seen you in jeans."

"Well, I've never seen you with blonde hair, but certainly you don't think I wear business suits and skirts twenty-four hours a day?"

"No, of course not. It was just ... startling. So, did you want to order something or just get down to business? I wouldn't bother with the coffee."

"I'm not hungry. I'd rather just get to the point here. I'm on vacation and being out here ... exposed like this, I don't like it."

"Fair enough."

"I just want to say upfront, I'm not here for you. This is a favor to Ollie."

"Ok." I had no illusions about how Dina would feel about doing this but I didn't expect immediate hostility. I guess I should be happy she's being frank about it. I won't have to read between the lines.

"I admit, there's a professional curiosity, considering what the truth could mean for the future of the company, but aside from that, I don't want to be a part of this."

"I understand. I shared some reluctance with Ollie about getting you involved, but he was persistent. So, how do you want to handle this?" I take a sip of my coffee and instantly regret it, placing the cup right back down on the table.

"I was thinking I'd get a room, up north of the St. Mary's river, place I've been before. Little individual cottages for privacy. It's a little remote but won't send up as many red flags in case anyone is tracking me. I'll check in around four o'clock today. You come to the room around five-thirty and we'll do the session, *after* you've done some recon of the building and the surroundings, make sure nothing is out of place."

"That sounds perfect. Is there anything I can do to prep for this?"

"Not really. Just keep an open mind. You'll need to be as relaxed as you can possibly be, so just keep your mind space as calm as you can for the rest of the day. You spot anything unusual during recon, or even between now and then, we abort."

"Agreed. Sure you don't want a piece of pie or something?"

Dina has always stayed entirely professional with me. That's her job, of course, as she can't afford to get too friendly with the people she psychoanalyzes for fear of losing her objectivity. I just wish I could have a real conversation with her as a regular person and not the company counselor. She never bites on that idea.

"I have to go," Dina says, keeping her distance as always. "I'll text the hotel information as soon as I have it." She rises from her seat. "Keep your eyes peeled and I'll see you later today."

"Thank you for doing this. I know it's an imposition."

"I just hope the results are worth the risk."

"Me too."

6

Once I received the details from Dina about the cottage location, I drove there immediately, arriving around two-thirty in the afternoon. With three hours to kill, I had plenty of time to scout out the location and the little nearby town. The whole area around the lake and its dozens of inlets serve as a weekend getaway destination for locals and vacationers. Cute area. I could spend a few weeks here relaxing, reading, floating on a raft. I wonder sometimes if I will ever get to a point where I can do that again. Right now, I'm almost afraid to close my eyes for five minutes without the fear of waking up with a gun in my face, or worse yet, not waking up at all.

The place she chose has a dozen little individual cottages just far enough away from one another for a good sense of privacy. It's also rural enough that there is only one road going east and west running to it.

I stopped at a diner in town for a side order of bacon and a better cup of coffee. There were a few locals, but in the late afternoon, traffic was scarce. I saw nothing out of the ordinary.

At the cottages, I walked around with a book in my hand like I was searching for a peaceful place to read. No one seemed to notice me. There are no security cameras anywhere, very little foot or road traffic, and the management keeps to themselves unless called upon. This should be the perfect location for what we need to do.

Truth is, if either Dina or myself are being actively tracked, there's nowhere we can hide anyway, but if not, this place will work out fine.

At four o'clock sharp, Dina pulled into the small lot of the management office, went inside to check in, and eventually made her way down to cottage 401. For unknown reasons, the cottages are numbered 401-412 and start numerically from east to west, the opposite of what one might expect.

I saw Dina passing glances around the area as she walked from the office to the car and from her car to the cottage. She was completely unaware I was watching her, which is good. That means I did my job. A question remains. Is someone watching me watching her? Not so far as I can tell.

Five-thirty finally arrives and I show up at the cottage door, knocking three times as we agreed via text. Dina answers, at first looking past me for any signs of trouble.

"We're alone," I say.

"Can't be too careful. Come in." Dina stands aside and lets me pass.

The cottage is quaint and country farm house themed. The kitchenette is decorated with roosters and a bar height bistro table. The living area has a full complement of tan leather furniture, a honey oak coffee table and matching end tables, and brass lamps with beige shades.

I walk immediately to the back of the cottage and find a master bedroom complete with king-sized, four poster bed and a luxury bathroom with clawfoot tub, and a second smaller bedroom and bath. I scan each room, looking behind every door to make sure I'm not being setup. The place is clear. I return to the main living area.

"Sorry, gotta protect myself."

"Understandable. Go ahead and take a seat on the couch," Dina points. "Can I get you a bottle of water or a diet cola?"

I step to the couch. "No thank you. I'm fine." I take a seat on the right side of the couch. I'm tense, more so than I thought I would be. This isn't even my healthy skepticism at work. Perhaps, I'm terrified of what I might find out. I'm certainly anxious at the idea of being completely vulnerable with Dina. I keep my mind mostly closed off to people, and for good reason, but under hypnosis she'll be in control and might hear things I would never reveal to anyone. But I'm here and I need her help. I have no choice but to trust in her professionalism.

Dina takes a seat in the chair adjacent to me. There is a computer tablet on the table in front of us. She grabs it and uses a USB passkey she's wearing on a lanyard around her neck to get access.

"So, how does this work? You wave a pendant in front of my face, I go into a trance, and then you make me cluck like a chicken?"

"If you don't take this seriously, it won't work," Dina scolds. "I have other things to do if you'd rather not."

"I'm sorry. I'm just nervous. I visited my family home recently, the one from right before my parents went missing. It has me rattled about what I might find out here."

"That's understandable. If you don't mind sharing, did you discover anything useful?"

From the back, left pocket of my jeans I pull out a folded piece of paper. I hand it over to Dina. Along the way down to Jacksonville, I stopped in a library and made a photocopy of the picture from Allister Coal, just in case something happened to the original.

She unfolds it and takes a long look at the image. After thirty seconds, she looks over to me, then back down to the photo. "You look a lot like your mother. This must be hard. I can't fathom what you must be feeling."

"It's tough. By all accounts, they were good people."

"I imagine you're being torn apart about the dichotomy of what you do for AWT and how that same thing tore your life apart."

Not that I should be surprised, but it sure didn't take long for Dina to get right into the psychoanalysis. She is who she is, of course. She can no more stop herself from doing it than I can consciously choose to have decaf in the morning.

"Yeah, it's crossed my mind a time or ten."

"Do you think it will be possible to reconcile that problem?"

"Honestly," I shake my head. "I don't know. I mean, most of the contracts that come through AWT are against some pretty awful fuckers."

"There hasn't always been such discretion exercised. Around the time Ollie and I came on board, we helped engineer a shift in that. For the most part, Madame K appeared to back up the new policy, but she has a sharp edge about her that won't dull easily. When that second training mission for you was manufactured, we stood against it but were overruled. Ultimately, all final decisions fall to her. The rift that exists at AWT right now really boils down to those policies, more so than being about you specifically. Of course, the question still remains. What exactly is so special about you that Madame K would try to steer around the norms we had established just to get you in?"

"What indeed?" I'm genuinely shocked to hear Dina divulge so much information. I don't think she's ever been so forthright in the entire time I've known her. She's scared. That's what this tells me. From my experience, when somebody shows all their cards like this, it's because they feel they have no other choice. Suddenly, I'm scared too.

"Well, we should probably get started," Dina says. "Just sit back and try to get as relaxed as you can, mind and body. I'm going to use the bathroom, leave you alone for a minute. Take the time to get your breathing under control and your mind focused." She hands the photo back to me. "I'd put that photo away and try to think of something very specific and peaceful." She rises. "Be back in a minute or two." She leaves the room.

I return the photo to my back pocket and settle into my

seat, leaning my head all the way back against the over-stuffed cushion.

I close my eyes and focus my breathing. I imagine myself sitting on the edge of a long dock, watching the sun rise, just like I've done hundreds of times in Baltimore. I can almost smell the sea. The sound of the water slapping against the edge of the dock enters my memory. I start counting, kind of like counting sheep. It's a technique I use to keep my mind on one thing. By the time I get to twenty, I'm calm and ready to go.

Dina returns, sits down, and wastes no time putting me in the proper state.

I feel like I'm in a dream, floating through the years of my life. I'm outside myself, aware, yet not entirely. I hear a soft voice from time to time, more like a whisper, guiding me.

... stay relaxed ...

I can't pinpoint a specific person or place but my surroundings are familiar.

... what is your earliest memory? ...

... from your childhood ...

I bounce through time.

"I'm like twelve years old standing outside the children's home but I know that's not my first memory."

... further back, much further ...

"I'm in bed, in the dark. I'm five. I'm crying."

... that's good ...

... why are you crying? ...

"I was just told I would never see my parents again. That place was my new home. I was devastated. I was so young. I could barely understand what was happening. No one would tell me what happened to my parents."

... try to go earlier ...

... before you got to the children's home ...

"I'm trying. I don't see anything. It's all black."

... don't try to see it ...

... feel it ...

"I'm sitting in the backseat of a car. I'm playing with a stuffed animal. My kitty. I'm scared."

... do you see anyone else? ...

"Yes. There are two women standing outside of the car. They're talking but I can't hear what they're saying."

... do you recognize them? ...

"Dr. Greenburg. She's wearing an ugly plaid skirt. I remember her wearing it all the time."

... what about the other woman? ...

"I can't see her face but she's familiar. I think she brought me there. I get out of her car, a big black car, and get into Dr. Greenberg's."

... good ...

... go back further ...

... earlier that day ...

"I'm in a room with two beds. And juice. I drink juice. It makes me sleepy."

... a hotel ...

... that's very good ...

... now follow yourself back to before the hotel ...

"I just woke up. I'm laying down in the backseat of the big black car. It's dark outside the windows. My head hurts. I find my kitty next to my leg."

... keep going ...

"I hear my mom. She's shouting at me to go brush my teeth. I don't want to. I stomp down the hallway toward the bathroom. Kitty is in my hand. I carry her everywhere."

... that's perfect ...

... go on ...

"In the bathroom. I put kitty on the toilet lid. There's a stepstool. I hop on it to brush my teeth. I grab my toothbrush. There's a noise from down the hall. A thud, like something big falling to the floor. I can feel my breathing change. I call to my mom. She doesn't answer."

... what are you feeling? ...

"I'm worried. I hear a strange sound, like short bursts of high-pressured air. I look into the mirror but past my own reflection and into the hallway behind me. There's a shadow there. It's moving toward me. My toothbrush drops into the sink."

... stay with it ...

... you're safe ...

... you won't be harmed ...

"At the doorway, a face emerges from the shadow of the hall. I can tell it's a woman but her mouth and nose are covered. Her eyes scare me most of all. She stops. I turn around on the stool. She doesn't move, just looks at me, like she doesn't know what to do. I ask her where's my mom. She stands silent."

... keep going ...

... you're doing great ...

"She pulls her mask down. It's then I see the gun in her other hand. I'm terrified. My leg and pants are suddenly wet."

... do you recognize the woman? ...

"No. I've never seen her before. But I know her now. She's ... she's ... rushing at me. I duck to the side and there's a quick snap of pain to the back of my head."

... you're okay ...

... can you see anything else? ...

"I can't. I'm so tired. So tired."

... you did great ...

... I'm going to countdown from five and when I reach the end, you're going to wake up ...

"Okay."

... five ...

... you're starting to wake up a little now ...

... four ...

... you're going to remember everything you saw ...

... three ...

... you're very relaxed ...

... two ...

... take a deep breath in and then out ...

... one ...

I open my eyes. I tilt my head forward to find Dina furiously taking notes on her tablet.

"How you feeling?" Dina asks.

"Tired. Depressed. Angry."

"That was quite intense. Can you ... remember everything? I took notes so I can refresh your memory."

"There's only one thing I need to remember, and that's Madame K killed my fuckin' parents."

My blood is at a low boil. If Madame K were in front of me right now, I'd jump up from this couch like a spider monkey and rip her apart with my bare hands.

"You're absolutely, positively sure it was Madame K herself?"

"Yes, I'm fuckin' sure," I snap. "I mean, she was much younger looking, but there's no mistaking those eyes. Eyes like she's seen some deep, dark shit."

"Oh, Josey. This is worse than I thought. I had no idea she was still pulling contracts herself at that time. But more importantly, why the hell did she keep you alive? That is out of character for her. There's a strict no witnesses policy in this line of work, and for good reason."

"I'm not sure I give two shits."

"I get that, but for the rest of us, it matters a great deal. You okay if I call Ollie and give him the info? We have to plan our next steps very carefully."

I nod. "Can I get one of those diet sodas you offered earlier?"

Dina rises, tablet in hand. "Help yourself to the fridge. I'll be back in a couple of minutes." She goes straight out of the front door, shutting it behind her.

I make my way to the kitchen and grab a can of soda. I pop the tab and chug half the damn thing. A few seconds later, I'm letting loose tiny burps. For some reason, it's helping to ease the tension. I giggle as I'm doing it. I suppose it's because I've always found bodily function noises hilarious.

I need this moment, this quiet, light-hearted moment. The dire path ahead of me will offer plenty of dark and bitter ones. Nothing good is going to come of all this drama thrust upon me. More people are likely to die. Hell, I'm probably going to end up dead. I can say for certain, I won't be going down without first setting the world on fire, if that's what it takes to avenge my parent's deaths. I could care less about why someone wanted them dead or whether they were ultimately good or bad people. They were my parents and they were taken from me, and me from them. And that requires a reckoning.

Pulling up that long-repressed memory of the day it happened and remembering that it was Madame K who actually pulled the trigger is more of a relief than it should be. I think the not knowing was the hardest part of all. I had some information. I could have simply held AWT as an organization responsible, and maybe that would have been enough. Knowing the killer, seeing her face, if only in a memory, gives my days going forward a lot more focus.

I'm standing here with the sense of an internal struggle developing. I've come to embrace my life as a paid assassin, and in some way, I've come to enjoy it. Admitting that leaves a dirty taste in my mouth, regardless, I see value in what AWT does. If only we could eliminate the collateral damage and the kinds of contracts that would destroy a family like mine. Amatto once told me that if I stick around long enough, I could be part of the generation that reshapes AWT into that vision many of us hold. Now, with the truth of my life revealed, I honestly don't know if that's possible.

Outside of the cottage ...

From a white wicker patio chair near the door of the cottage, Dina rubs her head to ease the emerging headache. Her position as behavioral therapist often comes with secondhand exposure to the worst of the worst from the assassin's game. With her involvement in the mystery that is Josey Baldwin, she finds herself on the front lines for the first time.

She's never felt scared for her own life until now. Hundreds of times she's helped AWT employees deal with the psychological effects of the job, but being on the opposite side of the barricade has left her anxious and needing a therapy session of her own.

Dina came outside to get some fresh air and make a phone call, but being out in the open is suddenly making her feel vulnerable. With trembling hands, she brings her phone to life using the fingerprint scanner on the back. She dials Ollie's number.

"How's it going?" Ollie asks.

"It's a ... to be honest, I'm terrified."

"What happened?"

"Well, we did the hypnosis and Josey remembered quite a bit, very specific. I feel bad for her. She was there when her parents were killed."

"I had a feeling. Did she actually see it happen?"

"No, but she did see the person responsible. It was Madame K. Way before our time, I guess when she was still doing contracts herself."

"Fuck. That was another thing I had a feeling about."

"Josey was in the bathroom brushing her teeth while her parents were being killed somewhere else in the house. She saw Madame K behind her in the mirror. That was the last thing she remembered before waking up in the backseat of a car. Shortly after that, she was handed over to Rosemary Greenburg."

"That's how I imagined it going down. I just don't get all that. Under normal circumstances, she would have had no choice but to kill the kid, and from what we know of her, she'd have no trouble doing it. So why didn't she?"

"That is *the* question in all this. We don't know why. Nothing Josey remembers explains why. We know who pulled the trigger but we still don't have the first clue as to the motivation."

"And whatever it is, I can't imagine it being so earth shattering that it would be worth killing or dying over."

Dina's attention is drawn to her right. From somewhere in the distance, there is subtle movement near another one of the cabins. With her eyes fixed in that direction, she continues listening to Ollie but is paying close attention to her surroundings. She rises from her chair.

"So, she let a witness live," Ollie says. "Big deal. Everybody fucks up now and again. Plus, that was in the early days when the kinks we're still being worked out."

Dina does not immediately respond. She's sweating. Her eyes cannot escape the place she saw movement moments before.

"Hello? Dina?"

"Yeah, sorry. I need to go inside. What do you think we should do?"

"Hang tight. Let me make a few phone calls. There's an APB out on Josey. If word gets back that anyone in the company is helping her, it won't be good."

"Okay. Thanks, Ollie. I gotta go."

"Okay," Ollie says, but Dina doesn't hear it.

She has already ended the call, pocketed her phone, and is through the door and back into the cabin. She finds Josey standing in the kitchen with a soda in her hand.

7

"If this call is about anything other than a confirmation that you have secured the target, I'm not going to be pleased," Madame K says.

"Pardon me, ma'am, but there's been a development," Ridge replies. He's standing against the west wall of cottage number 403. He's wearing khaki colored dungaree type pants, brown boots, and a dark brown button-up shirt under an even darker brown leather car coat. Hiding most of his pitch-black hair is a black wool cap. His full beard and moustache match his hair exactly. He's holding his cell phone in his left hand, a .45 caliber gun with a long silencer in the other.

"Get on with it."

"I've located the target. And she's with Dr. Whiteside."

"You're absolutely sure?"

"One hundred percent."

With zero hesitation, Madame K says, "Change order. Target now dead or alive. I also want Dina brought in, alive, preferably unmarked."

"Will do."

"Don't underestimate her. And don't fail me."

"I'll text when it's done."

8

"We need to leave," Dina says as she rushes through the doorway.

"Why? What happened?"

"I think I saw someone." She hurries over to the coffee table and gathers her materials, shoving them into her messenger bag.

"Who?"

"They know you're here."

"Shit. Are you sure?"

"I may not have your training, but I know when I'm being watched."

"Let's try to get to my car and we'll make a run for it." I pull a small pistol from around my ankle and hold it up for Dina to see. "This is all we got. The rest are in the car."

"Josey ... I'm scared," Dina reveals, dread filling her eyes.

I've never seen this side of her before – vulnerable, terrified. I start to take on some of her emotions myself. I need to push them aside. There is no place for them right now.

"Try not to worry. I'll get us out." It's a curious situation I find myself in, consoling Dina instead of the other way around. As much I hate being analyzed, I'd much rather we stay in our own lanes.

I take one last sip of the soda and place the can down on the counter. I go to the front window and peek around the left edge of the drapes.

"Get behind the couch and duck down," I instruct Dina.

She moves quickly and gets into position. Her breathing is shallow and quick.

"Did you see a man or a woman? How were they dressed?"

"I don't know. Ummm ... let me think. It was so fast. A man."

"Take a deep breath. I know you're nervous. What else?"

"He had on one of those black wool caps. And a full black beard. I'm pretty sure it was Ridge."

I turn to Dina. "Ridge?" I turn back to the window and look out a tiny slit. I don't see anyone and it's starting to get dark. I don't like this.

"He's a solo from AWT. Completely loyal to Madame K in a way you'll never be. He's dangerous."

"Great. Well, we need to move. We're just gonna run out of the front door straight to my car. Stay right behind me. Just do exactly as I say. If anything happens, just get down and stay out of sight. Okay?"

Dina stands up. "Okay."

I go to the front door and quickly throw it open. I pop my head out for one second to see if I can draw fire and gauge the direction Ridge is hiding out. A single shot penetrates the door jamb to my left. Phew. That was fucking close. This guy's reaction time is way faster than mine, but more importantly, I now know he's coming from the west.

I put a hand out for Dina. "Come on. We're going. Stay low."

She grabs my hand, and as fast as possible, we run while partially crouching down, leaving the cottage. Bullets whiz by as we run. We make it to the passenger side of my car.

"Get in the back," I instruct Dina.

As she does, I get in the front and slide over to the driver's side. As fast as I can, I put the keys in the ignition, start the car, throw it into REVERSE, and slam the gas pedal. Additional shots come at us, piercing the car's body and shattering the backseat driver's side window. I pay them no mind as I crank the steering wheel. The car whips around and I slam on the brakes. I throw the shifter into DRIVE and floor it. More bullets hit; the rear glass holds firm but is now riddled with holes.

I glance back at Dina. She's lying down on the seat, awkwardly holding her hands to her abdomen. Her bag has fallen off her shoulder and onto the floor, the strap still pinned to the inside of her left elbow joint.

"You okay?"

"Josey, I ... I," she stumbles to speak. She's crying, her lips trembling.

I keep driving, peeling out from the cottage property, heading east. Ridge will no doubt be following.

I look back again to Dina for the briefest of moments and see the blood pooling between her overlapping fingers. I'm struggling between wanting to stop and help her and continuing to drive. If we stop now, we're both dead. Ridge will catch up and finish us both. This is so fucked.

"Dina, just hang on." I accelerate even more, taking corners at dangerously high speeds, enough that if I'm not careful we're going to careen off the road and do Ridge's job for him in a rumbling, tumbling blaze of glory.

I grab my cell phone, Bluetooth in ear, and dial Ollie.

"Everything okay?" Ollie asks.

"We're fucked, Ollie. Fucked," I spit out. I can barely catch my breath to get the words out. I damn near veer off the road taking a corner too tight. Dina moans in discomfort. I keep glancing into the rearview mirror to check for Ridge. I don't see him. I don't know how anyone could keep up with me. At this pace, however, I'm going to end up in a police chase too.

"What the hell happened? Where are you?"

"With Dina." A let out a few hurried breaths. "In the car trying to get away from some asshole named Ridge."

"Oh shit, Josey. Shit, shit, shit."

"Yeah. Dina's been hit. I need a place to take her before

she bleeds out. Where do I go?"

"God-damn it! Don't let her die, Josey. Where are you?"

"I'm fuckin' trying. Heading west on 20, a few miles from Gainesville"

"Give me a sec."

"Hurry."

I slow down a little bit, thinking I've lost Ridge. It would be inconceivable for him to have caught up to me considering the head start and the random path I've been taking. I redirect the rearview mirror so I can see Dina. She's pale and not moving. The amount of blood startles me. I look away.

"Dina. Stay with me."

She doesn't respond or move in any way.

"I called Ollie. I'll get you help. Just stay with me."

"Josey?" Ollie chimes back.

"Help me, Ollie. Dina isn't doing too good."

"There's a hospital in the next town. You should be there in a minute or two."

"A hospital? That's not safe."

"We don't have a choice here. We have no assets close enough to help. Just go to the emergency room entrance, get her in a wheel chair, and get the hell outta there."

"I don't want to leave her, Ollie."

"No choice. Are you sure Ridge isn't onto you? You don't want to fuck with him."

"I lost him."

"Be sure."

"I'm sure." I almost want to cry thinking about Dina. "This is a total cluster fuck."

"Once you drop her off, you're going to need to get as far away from Florida as you can."

"I'll do my best. Shit, I see the hospital. I'll call you back when I'm clear." I don't even wait for a response and end the call.

I quickly find the emergency entrance and pull under the eave, just past the door.

I rush through the automatic double doors and straight to

the reception desk.

"My friend is in the back of my car and is bleeding out. I need people out there immediately or she's going to die."

I don't even let the woman behind the glass speak, I just turn back around, fly past the people in the waiting room, and out of the doors to my car. I open the passenger side rear door to find a motionless Dina, ghostly. I'm doing my best to focus but I feel like I'm on the edge of losing it.

To my left, three people wearing scrubs emerge from the doors and hustle over to me. The third is pushing a gurney.

I step back and let them exam Dina. They ask me questions but I don't answer, instead shaking my head, shock and dismay written all over my face. I'm faking all this so I don't have to explain that she was shot by an assassin or that I too am an assassin. It crosses my mind that perhaps I'm not faking. The last thirty minutes have been pretty fucking shocking.

They have Dina on the gurney but she is clearly unconscious. I hear the taller male nurse ask me to follow them in. He removes the lanyard from around Dina's neck and hands it to me, tells me to hang on to it. I suddenly remember my predicament.

"I'll move the car and meet you in there." I slam the car door.

He starts to shake his head, then waves me off. He catches up to the other two as they enter the building.

I hurry around the car and hop in. I didn't even realize I had left the keys in and left it running.

I drive for twenty minutes before my heart just won't let me go another mile. I pull off the road below an overpass.

I stare out of the windshield and lose all track of time. Suddenly, from deep within, an anger swells and works its way into my hands. My fingers slowly curl into my palms. I pound the steering the wheel with both fists six times, leaving them bloodied and bruised. A long, primal scream escapes my mouth, followed by a shorter, less intense one. I throw my head back, sobbing uncontrollably. I put my hands to my face, which is now hot and soaked in tears.

When I settle down, the real shit unfolds in my mind. There is no way Dina survived. She was likely dead long before I even arrived at the hospital. Oh ... the guilt. Strangely, Dina's voice is the one that pops into my head.

"I know you understand this can't possibly be your fault."

"If I hadn't gotten you involved, you'd still be alive."

"Maybe, but you didn't pull the trigger. That was Ridge. He made choices too."

"That's too simplistic and you know it."

"Of course it is. But we all signed up to work in a dangerous profession. Even the so-called office grunts like me are at risk. Eventually, the odds run out for all of us."

"I don't think I can do this anymore. I don't want to do this anymore."

"Well, I don't know if they'll just let you walk away. There are people they could hurt to get to you."

An idea crosses my mind. Where could I go that would allow me to monitor the Leer family yet stay hidden? I could hide in plain sight, in Baltimore, that's where. Never in a million years would the organization think I'd be so stupid as to return there. Then again, I'm using a little reverse psychology here. They may just think to reverse-reverse it. Maybe I can count on Ollie to steer them away from that idea, assuming he still has any kind of influence over the situation.

My thoughts return to Dina. I now realize how valuable she was to me, and to the company. She didn't always give us the answers we wanted, only the ones we needed, and she sure as hell had a knack for asking just the right questions that would inevitably lead to us discovering some truth or solution ourselves. Even gone, she still managed to psychoanalyze me. Damn, she was good.

9

Six days later – August 20th

Like the worst fucking movie cliché in the world, the day of Dina's funeral arrives along with gray skies and a light mist. I've ditched the car and found another one, actually quite similar but different enough that it won't be on anyone's radar. Ollie warned me to get as far away from the situation as possible when we last spoke but I just couldn't run away without saying goodbye.

In my pursuit for answers to the shitstorm known as My Past, someone I trust, perhaps one of only a handful, has gotten caught up in the wake. I'm having trouble rising each day without immediately self-medicating. The pain and guilt – they're crippling. It's one thing for some asshole wannabe gangster or lowlife criminal to get tossed into the blackhole of my world and end up dead, but when innocent people get tangled up in it just for being near me, that I can't seem to reconcile.

Don't get me wrong, I was not a fan of Dina's role as team psycho-analyst, but I sure as hell respected her as a person, and she sure as hell didn't deserve to die.

I didn't pull the trigger, and I constantly hear her voice telling me that, but when I close my eyes and see her ghostly, near lifeless face, her bloodied hands, lying helpless in the backseat of my car, I can only see my own responsibility in this mess. I want to blame this Ridge asshole. I want to blame Dina and Ollie for even recruiting me in the first place. I want to blame Madame K for changing my history and thus staging my future. Today, however, as the weather and the circumstances cast clouds and gloom over everything, I blame only myself.

In the backseat of the car where Dina died, I did find and keep her bag, a bag with a few personal items and her tablet, the tablet she used to take notes about my hypnosis session. I suddenly remember the lanyard I have in my pocket. I debate whether or not I should be snooping around her stuff but curiosity gets the best of me. I boot up the tablet and use the passkey. There are folders on the desktop, each named by year. I choose one at random and start to read the written musings of Dina Whiteside, this file labeled as being about a year into her tenure at AWT.

In the world of contract assassination, there are layers of trust - invisible walls that can be perceived but rarely broken. These inherent mental devices allow for some semblance of safety, or else, perhaps, no one in the business could possibly get a single night's peaceful sleep.

There too is the ability to compartmentalize, as all humans find an expert-level penchant for at some point in life. This may be even more important for those living in these shadows of blood and death. (Is this how I really see this world already? As blood and death? I find that discouraging)

Compartmentalizing, specifically, in regards to the collateral damage that often comes with the territory, though avoided whenever possible, is of key interest to me. Over time, it seems to wear down the soul of even the most brutish. Helping these assassins to find a mind space where the lives they take and damage can be tucked away is going to be essential. And while we do have the ability to bury some things very deep in order to keep functioning, I do believe there is a limit. I tend to think of compartmentalizing in physical terms, so just like a closet, our minds only have so much space for this function.

On the issue of trust, there exists a massive paradox that everyone acknowledges but rarely speak of. In this business of secrets and covert operations, there must be a high level of trust placed in the people of AWT, the ones that accept and plan the missions, the ones who provide Tech Ops, in me, yet the kind of individuals we recruit tend to inherently have trust issues. The perfect recruit cannot be the perfect recruit without having dealt with the kind of life experiences that destroy faith in other people. Balancing this simple truth will likely be my greatest challenge here.

I'm left with two big questions:

How much mental space is available to the average assassin for storing away the horror, the pain, the death, the empathy?

What happens when the trust in AWT and the leadership is fractured?

All the major players from AWT are present today to say goodbye to their coworker and friend. They've taken heavy precautions in the matter of security. They have arranged for the rest of the cemetery to be closed. They have armed guards present at key locations on and around the property. They even barricaded all entrances and exits.

I'm a few hundred yards away in the woods of a nearby property. I'm forced to view this entire thing through high-powered binoculars. I will make an attempt to visit the gravesite, probably right after they all leave. I don't think they would expect that, and I'll have to be quick. They'll have eyes all over this place for several days, hoping to catch me. I would just as soon not let that happen.

I honestly can't see how the company could possibly function without Dina. She's the barometer by which all of us measure the air in the room, and while no one is truly neutral, she is the closest thing we had to such a thing. With Dina gone, I fear whatever power struggles are going on at AWT will only escalate. What that means for me is unknown. If I had to guess, I'd say my life just became expendable.

I grab the binoculars and focus in on the group seated under the tent. I scan the faces and the one missing person from AWT, aside from Ridge, is Amatto. He could be on security detail or on some mission. Who knows? He's the company's number one asset. The one thing I still don't know is how many solo assassin types AWT employs? This Ridge guy appears to be another one. They are the assassins I need to be on the lookout for. They're the ones that will be hunting me. Ridge had a chance and failed. I doubt that will be his only attempt.

The front row of people nearest the gravesite are faces I don't know at all. I assume they are Dina's family members. Madame K, Li Xia, Greg, Nazir, and a few others from AWT are seated in the second row. Ollie, not surprisingly, is standing at the back of the tent, all the way in the corner, as far away from Madame K as a person could be under that shelter. He may have been relegated to last-line security, but my guess, he doesn't want to be anywhere near the queen bee.

Looking at the faces of the AWT people, I don't see humans and their emotions, I see killer robots, devoid of feeling. I've met these people, some more intimately than others, so I know it's not true, but I can't help seeing them in this way. I will be blamed for Dina's death. That means everyone at the company is now my enemy. Madame K won't have it any other way.

For an hour, I watch the funeral service, and finally, the graveside procession. Madame K is the first of AWT to leave in her car. Once the family and everyone else is gone, Ollie and The Dean are all that remain. They are conversing. I wish I could hear what they're saying. My ears are burning, so I assume it's about me.

*

Between Ollie and The Dean (aka Li Xia)

"Glad we have a minute to talk, Li," Ollie says. "This last week has been something else."

"Yes. We have to tread carefully. My most recent chat with Madame K actually pushed me into a more definitive position on this uprising of yours."

"Oh? Do tell."

"I flat out asked her if she had considered that it might be time for a regime change."

"Jesus, Li! Are you fuckin' crazy?"

"She agreed to give me a safe conversation. I took her at her word. I knew it was a risk, but I needed her to give me something. Body language, a telling remark, anything."

"I hope you got what you wanted. So, where do you stand?"

"I'm with you. My impression was that she has no intention of stepping down and she'll go to the grave fighting any attempt to take her down."

"I figured as much." Ollie releases a deep sigh. He glances over to the gravesite of Dina. "We're down one ally, and she had the most insight of all of us into the mind of the boss. Do we really have a chance now?"

"Probably not. But can we really continue on? There is no confidence left in the leadership direction. Time has made her unstable and unreliable. That is a dangerous combination in someone with so much power, especially in this line of work. Aside from that, there is still the issue of Josey Baldwin. The status quo means taking her down. I know how you feel about her."

Ollie begins to pretend a denial but relents with a nod.

"Will you be prepared to handle that task if it came down to you being the trigger man?"

"Honestly, doubtful. She's not to blame for this mess. Madame K is. We are. She doesn't deserve any of this."

"Then I guess there is only one thing left to do."

"We're going to need a plan."

"I have some ideas. One thing is certain. We'll have to get her away from headquarters, isolate her, otherwise, she'll have the tactical advantage."

"Until then, we have to be cautious, play the game, and soften up the tone around the building."

"Agreed," Li Xia says as she looks one last time at the grave of her friend and co-worker. Though she won't show it on the outside, the death of Dina has her riddled with fear and anger.

"Let's get the hell outta here," Ollie says.

They part ways, walking separately to their cars.

*

After a long conversation, Ollie and Li Xia finally leave. I'll still have to wait a few minutes before I head over to the gravesite. My best guess is the AWT stooges assigned to watch this place for the next few days will leave for a few hours, then return to keep an eye out for me. I'll be long gone by the time they show up.

As I sit here killing time, I can't help but wonder what the atmosphere must be like at headquarters. A rogue assassin. A dead therapist. A dead, backstabbing Kill Team member and a crippled one. A psychotic boss. A possible uprising. Sounds like a pyramid now sinking into the sand. I do not envy them.

I watch the cemetery employees backfill the plot using a small orange and black tractor. They break down the pop-up canopy, fold up the chairs, and finally, roll up the fake green turf and haul it all away in the trailer attached to the tractor.

I walk a long circular pattern around the perimeter of the cemetery, circling inward as I go, constantly checking in all directions for bogeys.

I notice my steps slowing as I come upon the final resting place of Dina. The grassy, musty odor of recently upturned soil wafts through the air. Even after some time, I'm still getting hints of perfume from one of the women that attended.

About five feet away, I stop near the plot and wonder why I feel the need to be here at this moment. I wasn't all that close to Dina, not to mention, every second I hang around, I'm at significant risk. Then it hits me, like a brick to the face. The sting fills my eyes instantly with tears.

Guilt.

Regret.

I crumble to my knees, crying so uncontrollably, my chest hurts and I can't refrain from wailing aloud, despite the fact I shouldn't be doing anything that might draw attention. I simply can't stop. All the pent-up emotion, all the pain, all the heartbreak, erupts into a seriously ugly cry. Glad I'm not looking in the mirror and that no one else is around.

After calming down a little, I pull my head out from between my knees and look right at the fresh mound of dirt in front of me.

"There's nothing I can say that will make this okay. I fucked up. I don't know if you'd be happy to hear it, but I'm done."

I use the sleeve of my hoodie to wipe my nose and my hand to dry my eyes.

"I don't have all the answers I want and need, but whatever the truth is, it's not worth more people dying over. So, I'm out."

I take a glance around and find nothing out of the ordinary, but my internal danger clock is ticking faster and faster.

"I will probably be pursued forever, so I'm just going to have to find a hole to crawl into and disappear. Jesus, that was a bad metaphor considering where I'm at. I think you'd understand. I've never been all that tactful. And I'm selfish. I'll work on that.

"I have to leave." I get on my feet, dust myself off, and pull the hoodie over my head. "If you're somewhere psychoanalyzing dead people in the ethereal realm, I hope you can forgive me for getting you involved in my bullshit, and I'm sure I'm destined to end up on your couch at least one more time."

I step around a few headstones to get back to the path, then jog back to my entry point, hopefully working out the rest of the tension in my body.

Back at my car, I arrive slightly out of breath and feeling much better. All I can think about is getting the fuck out of Florida. I don't know where I'll end up. Right now, I'm going to pop into Baltimore, probably for the last time, then I'll vanish.

10

Madame K's Office

Ridge's years of training and experience led him to paranoia. Once inside Madame K's office, he stands with his back against the wall, right next to the entry door. In any situation, he refuses to have a door at this back. Even in the highly secure headquarters of AWT and in the office of the boss, the rule still applies.

He stands six-feet one inch tall, slightly muscular, grizzled, tan, beard and mustache kept at the five o'clock shadow phase. His demeanor suggests calm and indifference. His appearance speaks of a man that would just as soon snap your neck as shake your hand.

Ridge did not want to be anywhere near headquarters. He had, in fact, only stepped foot on the property three other times in the last four years. He has become a self-reliant, efficient, calloused assassin with no taste for corporate bullshit. After the Florida debacle, he longed for it that much less, but he knew his failure would require some in-person ass kissing of the highest order.

Madame K sits behind her desk, nursing a vodka tonic, her mind still reeling from the Dina situation. She has remained mostly calm, considering the circumstances, but at some point, she is bound to explode.

Ridge is silent, staring in Madame K's general direction but mostly looking past her to the view of the city.

Madame K stays silent too, letting an uncomfortable amount of time pass before deciding to speak. Even without Dina, the psychological renderings appear nonetheless.

"Josey Baldwin has made a fool of you, and by extension, of this company and of me."

Ridge does not respond. He knows better than to speak in a situation of this sort without being asked to. For the moment, he buries his ego.

"This was sloppy. I don't quite know how to proceed with this matter. You have any thoughts on that before I decide?"

Ridge rubs his bristled chin, contemplating the kind of answer he wants to give. There are no good options, only ones that will hurt a little less than others.

"Not like I was after some dirty fuckin' accountant here. She's trained for this shit, same as me. Dina was ... an unfortunate accident."

"YOU," Madame K shouts while slamming her open hand on the desk, "have been doing this for a long time," she goes on, firm and staccato. "SHE ... is a fucking child by comparison."

Ridge fights hard not to blowup in response to the questioning of his abilities. He chooses to be contrite.

"You're right. I underestimated her. I was too confident. I was fairly certain she didn't even know I was there."

"You can be a difficult person to deal with at times. But you've also been a great asset."

With her left hand, Madame K picks up her glass, takes a sip, and places the glass back down, all without breaking direct eye contact with Ridge. Her right hand has moved to her lap.

"I mean, I never cared much for Dina, but I had no reason or desire to see her dead. What can I do to rectify the situation? You put me out there again to get Josey, it will be done, period."

The words of Ridge settle into Madame K's brain in only the negative spaces. She needs some sort of justice for Dina's death. Josey seeing her end would satisfy that need, but she has doubts, and to Madame K, it feels too far away to placate her current anger.

She takes in a long, deep breath, grips the pistol in her lap with a finger on the trigger, exhales, and then, as the last of the air escapes her lips, she raises the gun and takes aim.

Ridge's eyes widen. He has no weapon on him for defense. They are not allowed in Madame K's office. Her doorway has a built-in metal detector. He reaches to his right to find the doorknob.

Madame K presses the trigger only once. The shot passes right through Ridge's left eye socket. The bullet explodes out of the back of his head and lodges itself into the wall behind him.

His outstretched arm falls back to his body. The noise was minimal, the suppressor doing its job.

She wonders if he remained conscious long enough to see her face with his other eye as she smiled, happy with the accuracy of the shot and relieved that someone paid a price for Dina.

A few moments later, his body slumps to the floor, falling slightly toward and into the pathway of the door.

Madame K gently places the gun on a folded copy of the Wall Street Journal on her desk. She then presses the intercom button on her desk phone.

"I need a Level C cleanup crew in my office, immediately. Also, call my car and driver up to the deck. I'm going out."

"Right away, ma'am."

11

The streets of Baltimore are quiet at two a.m. Most of my time here in the past was spent during these dark hours. All the good shit happens after ten around here. There exists a strange dichotomy where the streets and sidewalks seem abandoned but the warehouses, alleys, overpasses, and back lots are teeming with activity. I have no intention of going that route. I just happened to get into town at this hour and it's bringing back memories.

I'm a different person now. Not better, certainly not above it. I suppose I've simply graduated. The low-level crap going on down here was like a run through the minor league baseball system, but now I'm in The Show. That other Josey feels like a lifetime ago. Doesn't really matter. I'm not here for that crap anyway.

Hiding. In plain sight. That's what I'm doing. I need to find a place to lay low until I can figure out a more permanent solution to my bigger problems. AWT has all the resources in the world, and if the full power and money of the company were spent on the endeavor, they'd find me, eventually. That ain't happenin'.

For now, I've decided to stay away from the Leer Family, although, there will be a daily temptation to just pop over there. I won't. It's way too dangerous. The company may even be smart enough to have eyes on them.

Someone I do intend to see is Sake Tom. My lifesaver. My mentor. My friend. Even in our short time together, he became the closest thing I've ever had to a father figure. I didn't see it or appreciate that fact at the time, but I understand it now. He helped to make me aware yet not scared, he taught me to defend myself in ways I couldn't conceive, and he's the one who made me care about other people for the first time.

Before meeting Tom, I had never experienced another human being doing anything that wasn't completely self-motivated. He took me in, trained me in self-defense and the art of being invisible, and in the end, he got nothing else from it other than having someone to talk to. What Tom saw was someone who needed his special kind of help, so he helped. That is the number one thing I took with me. After that, whenever I saw a woman in distress or being taken advantage of, I used my skillset to make things right. As I sit here and think about it, in some way, my training and work as an assassin is really just an extension of that mentality. Dina sold me on the altruistic nature of the paid assassin, the leveling of an unfair playing field. I've never seen my own life's overall progression in this way before now. Interesting.

Thinking of Dina reminds me of her journals, so I decide to take another glimpse into her mind. I bring out her tablet and find another random file to read.

My first eighteen months at AWT has flown by. There has been very little for me to complain about. I get along well with the leadership group, especially Ollie. We seem to align on most important issues, he's direct, and I trust him. That part doesn't come easy, not for anyone around here. In this business, it can't be helped that there is a constant undercurrent of mistrust that runs beneath the handshakes, the smiles, and the nods. Somehow, we all manage to keep our minds right despite the paradoxical feelings. Some of us are probably better at it than others. Our backgrounds are as varied as the average family diner's menu, yet there is one thing we all seem to have in common – a past filled with a kind of questionable behavior that polite society cannot rationalize, accept, or believe.

My own story might be a bit less complicated and devious as the rest, but obviously, there must be something about me. I do have a certain moral haziness that has no basis in social norms or religiosity. That's a great stepping stone for this business. Usually, it's not enough, I'm discovering, but for my position as team counselor and academy recruiter, I guess it's okay.

I do miss teaching. The university atmosphere is incomparable to any other when it comes to work. For a professor, there's a powerful intoxication present in molding young minds, shaping their thoughts and future behaviors. The problem came from my fierce independence for reasonable thought and discourse. That doesn't always go well with college-aged people who easily latch on to causes with little wisdom or perspective.

I had gone through a few interesting periods where some students rebelled against even discussing certain topics with objective hindsight. I stayed afloat but the writing was on the wall. My time, at least at this particular university, was nearly up. Lucky for me, someone I didn't know at all had come to see me speak at a symposium on the topic of wrong and right, and how there is no such thing as either.

I noticed him standing at the back of the auditorium, obscured from above by the shadows of the upper deck. He was wearing a business suit that I could guarantee was the most expensive one in the room. For the entire forty-five-minute speech, he leaned up against the wall with his arms crossed, never moving once. After a brief Q&A at the end, the audience left but he stayed put.

As I reached the end of the center aisle to leave, without even looking over at me, he spoke.

"I'm surprised you haven't been run out of here yet."

I stopped and faced him. "It won't be long." I let out a nervous laugh. "My master plan to get released from my tenure with a massive payout is almost complete."

"For the record, I happen to agree with your take on right and wrong. Perspective is everything."

"Thank you for saying that. I think we're in a significant minority on that one."

He finally turned to face me. "You have no idea." He pulled a business card from a pocket on the inside of his suit coat and walked over to me with his hand out. "Should your master plan come true and you wish to continue working, but maybe for a company that appreciates your reasonable attitude and flexible take on ethics, call that number and ask for Ollie. We might have something for you."

I took the card but didn't think much of it at the time. I thanked him and told him I would consider it. I shoved the card in my bag without even looking at it. I didn't actually expect to lose my job or ever feel pressured enough to leave. Boy was I wrong.

Three months later, after another group of students reported me to the university administration for daring to engage in a conversation that suggested bad genetics or mental illness could be possible sources for transgender people being the way they are, I was given an ultimatum. No more of those kinds of discussions on campus or they'd have no choice but to boot me. I went home so pissed off, I didn't think I'd ever return to campus. I did, for about two weeks, until I found the card Ollie had given me.

I remember staring at the card and thinking how it must be a joke. What kind of company hands out business cards with nothing on them, save for a phone number hand written in black ink? No name, no company, no logo. It was weird but I called anyway right there from my office at the college.

I went through the whole cloak and dagger thing. The blindfold, the black SUV with tinted windows, a two-hour drive to an unknown location. Honestly, it scared the crap out of me. My first meeting at AWT was with Li Xia and Ollie. They gave me the whole rundown and I was astonished, to say the least.

The world to me had suddenly become foreign, like a far-off place you might read about in a book but would never visit. I couldn't go anywhere after that meeting without looking over my shoulder, being instantly aware of suspicious individuals, scared of every sound that reminded me of gunfire. I had barely stepped foot in the lifestyle, but this hour-long interview and secret rendezvous had left me shaken, my reality altered forever. Ironically, I had suddenly become in need of a psychologist to help temper my reaction. I was certain my interviewers could see it written all over my face.

I left feeling like I didn't perform well at the impromptu interview, but they called me back a day later and I returned for a final interview, this time with Madame K. She pulled no punches about what she would expect of me. She spoke eloquently, firmly, and directly. I appreciated her honesty but she also scared me. I had no doubts she was no one to be trifled with.

I was given a job offer right then and there. The salary was nearly ten times my university pay but I was terrified to get into this industry. Going to jail and getting killed are very real consequences of being in that building, in any capacity. My intellectual curiosity, however, seemed to have forced my hand.

Now, here I am getting close to my two-year anniversary with the company, pondering my development as a psychologist and as a human being. The concept of right and wrong comes up often in this business, not openly, mind you, but I know some of us marinate on the philosophical parts of this line of work from time to time.

I do see value in what we do. I get all the arguments, from all sides. What right does anyone have to engage in such acts of wanton aggression against another person? Maybe none, but the truth is, human beings have been doing this exact thing in one form or another since the beginning of civilization. War is a type of mass assassination, if you think about it. How many people have been killed historically, especially innocent ones, during acts of war? In our line of business, we at least take care to minimize collateral damage, if not avoid it completely. And we operate on such a small scale, our work could be seen as relatively insignificant, like the Earth as one of billions of planetary bodies amongst the stars of our Milky Way galaxy.

There might just be a small part of me that keeps coming back to these arguments, as if I am not totally convinced that what we do is acceptable. Perhaps that is a consequence of my social programming.

Perhaps it is the natural guilt and empathy I feel for other human beings. It could very well be that we are indeed wrong in our behaviors and my mind must constantly tell me otherwise in order to stay sane. One thing is for certain – there is a lot to explore on this topic and I relish the opportunity to do so.

12

I awoke this morning from a surprisingly restful night's sleep. A fluffy bed in a five-star hotel doesn't hurt. A corner room on the top floor doesn't hurt either. No one at AWT would suspect me staying at a place like this. We do seedy roadside motels with thin walls and gravel parking lots. We don't do concierge and valet. Well, at least not while we're trying to stay hidden.

I traded my shitty car for an even shittier burgundy minivan this morning, my third new vehicle in a week. The rusty bottom edge is particularly nice. After filling up the beast with petrol, I drive to the old neighborhood where I first met Tom.

I park a block down from his house. In the years since I left this area, the environment has only gotten worse. The streets have more potholes, the buildings are seemingly even more crumbly, and there are more broken-down cars around than there are trees. Sad.

As I walk, my memories of these roads begin to emerge but I hold the emotional edge and my fears at bay. My training and experiences have my confidence at an all-time high. The large blade and two guns on my person don't hurt either, not to mention the fact it's 10:30 in the morning.

When I hit the corner of the property, I get a little feeling of disappointment. Tom was meticulous about how his house looked, and his yard especially. The chain-link fence leans inward in several spots and the yard is full of weeds and ten inches tall in places. My first thought is that he can't possibly be living here anymore.

Regardless, I go through the gate, up the porch, and after a deep breath, knock hard five times on the fading white door.

Twenty seconds roll by and just as I'm thinking about knocking again, I hear the chain slide and the two other locks click.

The door opens and before me stands a six-foot tall, rail thin black woman wearing baby blue scrubs. Her skin is flawless. She's definitely older than me but she could be forty or she could be sixty.

"Can I help you?" she asks.

"Yeah. I'm sorry. I'm looking for someone that used to live here. He's an old friend."

"Well, I don't live here, honey. I'm taking care of the man who does. Who's the person you're looking for?"

"Tom Ichiro. It's been a few years."

"Ooooohhh ... he's still here. How do you know him?"

I have to think about that for a moment. How do I sum up my relationship with Tom? I've never had to before now.

"He was a mentor of mine. Helped me through some tough shit, pardon my language, when I lived around here."

"So, I take it you're here to say goodbye? Well, come on in then. I'm his main hospice nurse Shantelle. What's your name honey?" She steps aside, ushering me through the doorway and past her into the living room.

"Josey."

I enter but my steps are weighted in confusion. Hospice? Like dying hospice? I'm simply not prepared to hear that. I need a drink.

Shantelle closes the front door and turns to me. "Just let me check on him and tell him you're here, Josey."

"Hey, ummm ... what kind of condition is he in? Like,

does he have cancer or something?"

"He has good days and bad days but he is mentally sharp. As for his illness, you'll have to ask *him*." She puts up her right index finger. "Just give me a sec."

I nod.

She hustles from the room and down the hallway.

With my arms at my sides, I twiddle and flex my fingers like I'm attempting to get more blood flow to them. The truth is, my brain is what needs more blood flow. I can't seem to form a cohesive thought.

I'm not even over Dina's death and five seconds after getting into Baltimore I find out Sake Tom is dying. I don't know if I can deal with this shit right now. I might just crack.

It's weird. I can almost feel myself going through the stages of grief while I'm standing here waiting. I started to tell myself this can't be happening, but that was quickly erased and replaced with a pissed off internal *fuck this shit*. I even started to think that maybe money was the issue and that I could somehow pay for more treatments that might save him. And this whole thought process happened in mere seconds. Now, I'm sad, and all those other things are just hovering around. So instead of stages, it's a big bowl of shitty soup that was just dumped on my head. A part of me wishes I hadn't come.

Shantelle returns. "You want a bottle of water? That's all there is. The room can get hot."

"I'm fine. Thanks."

"I'll wait out here so you can have some privacy. Last room on the left."

"Thank you."

Shantelle sits down in the chair closest to the front door and immediately starts messing around on her phone.

I walk down the hallway and find Tom's room open. I step into the door frame and wait there.

Tom is already looking my way and when he sees me, he smiles.

His bedroom is mostly like it was the last time I saw it,

except his bed has been replaced with a hospital-style one and there's an oxygen machine. The bed is up at a thirty-degree angle and he has two pillows stuffed behind his shoulders, neck, and head.

"Don't be shy. Get in here. I'm not contagious. I'm just dying. Perfectly normal."

Tom always had a way of being curt but comforting. Insert your favorite cliché here.

I walk over to his bedside, forcing a sad smile.

He takes my hand. "I knew I would see you again. I wish it were under better circumstances."

"I'm sorry I haven't been by. Life has been ... killer." The joke is lost on Tom. I'm cracking up in my head.

"Don't apologize to me. You owe me nothing. I just hope life is treating you well. Tell me what you've been up to. And don't leave out the juicy bits. Nurse Morphine won't tell me jack-shit."

"Hey! She seems nice and is taking care of you."

"I know, I know. I'm just playing my role as the grumpy, dying old bastard."

I shake my head.

"I don't know about juicy bits, but things have been crazy, that's for damn sure."

"What kind of work are you doing?"

"The kind that would put your life in danger if you knew too much about it."

He stares me down, cocks his head. He believes me and I can see it worries him. "In case you can't tell, I don't have much life left. So, what could be the harm?"

He does have a point. Worst case scenario, he's carried out of the house a few days early. Might be merciful, depending on the state of his body, which I have no intention of even asking him about. If he brings up his illness, I'll certainly listen, but otherwise, I don't want the gory details.

"To be honest, I don't want to tell you. You'll be disappointed and possibly infuriated."

"You always had a fire in your belly. I didn't exactly think you'd become a nun."

"More like the exact opposite."

"Ahhhh ... a politician then." He nods a few times.

I chuckle. "Not that evil. Well, maybe. Depends on how you look at it."

Tom throws his head back against his pillow with his eyes closed, grimacing.

"Shit, are you okay? Tom? I'll get Shantelle."

I start to turn around but he grips my hand tighter so I can't move.

Tom opens his eyes and slowly reveals a smile.

"You should see the look on your face. Priceless." He laughs hysterically.

I use my free hand to slap the top of his hand that is still in my grip. "You fucker! That is cruel."

"I can't take this anymore. Everyone gets so serious when you're dying." He exhales.

"I get it, but that was still mean you old fucker."

"I haven't laughed that hard in years. So, come on. I've got a week or two, at best. Tell me the truth."

"Okay, okay. Where to start? A few years ago, I was approached by a woman who claimed the company she worked for had been watching me, and they decided I was a prime candidate for a training program call the Kill Academy."

"Kill Academy? I'm guessing that's not just a clever name but something more literal?"

To my surprise, Tom's question and his facial expression are of deep curiosity, and not judgment, as I thought they would be.

"Quite literal. I reluctantly accepted and spent several months training to be an assassin. They grouped us into three-person teams with two assassins and one tech person. We eventually moved into a highly-secured house together and did several contracts as a team.

"Now, before you say anything, the company is really strict about the contracts they take. No children, of course, but they try to take contracts where the target is a shitty person. They consider it a kind of balancing of the scales of justice. I bought in. Now, I'm not so sure. I'm on the run. Sooooo much shit has gone down. You can never tell anyone I was here."

"Is your life in danger? Did you come here to hide?" Tom asks with genuine concern in his voice. He even sounds a little scared. I don't think I've ever heard him scared.

"Very much in danger. I'm attempting to hide in plain sight. Not here, in your house per se, but around. I just wanted to see you again. I don't know where I'm going to end up after this."

"I don't need to tell you how much I don't like this idea of you killing people for money."

"I knew exactly how you'd feel about it. But the money. Phew, it's really good. Well, it was. I don't have much of it left honestly. I could only take so much when I bailed."

Tom coughs gently with his lips closed. He puts up his index finger, turns his head, and then coughs vigorously for a good twenty seconds. His hand goes up to let me know he's okay.

"You want me to get the nurse?"

He shakes his head. "I'm alright." He clears his throat. "I'm fine."

He turns back to me and grabs the sweating glass of water from his nightstand. He takes a few shallow sips before returning it to the coaster.

"Ugh. Heart disease," Tom huffs out. "What no one understands ... until they go through it ... is how connected the heart and the lungs are."

"That's what's getting you? Heart disease? Wouldn't have bet on that one. So, it's hard to breathe?"

"Most of the time. The first thing in your body that fails after a heart attack is your lungs, aside from the heart, of course."

"When did that happen? The heart attack, I mean?"

"The last one was almost two years ago."

"Ex-squeeze me? Last one?"

"My third. The first was years ago when I still ran the restaurant. The second was a few years before we met."

"You never mentioned it."

"Not exactly something that comes up in casual conversation. I survived and wasn't too bad off, but the third one came the closest to killing me. Well, in some way, it will kill me, it's just taking a couple of years."

"I'm really sorry, Tom. This sucks. I don't know what to say."

"You said hello. Now say goodbye. I've had a good run and a long life."

Tom grabs my hand, holds on tight, and continues, "I don't know what happens when a person dies, but I hope I get to see my Fumi again. And my parents if they're not too busy. And before the end, I'm happy I got to see you again too. You reminded me of what life is really all about. We have to pass on what we know so that others can benefit from our experiences."

I can't help but cry a little. I use my free hand to cover my eyes and then wipe the moisture away. I can't bear to open them, to see his face, and acknowledge his end. I can hear him sobbing too.

I squeak out a *goddamn it* and finally look at him again. We cry together for what seems like forever, and when we finally stop, we laugh a little at how ugly the tears got. Maybe it was just to ease the tension.

"Thank you for that," Tom says. "I think I needed it. I've balled a few times recently but never with anyone around. I don't have anyone."

"Oh, Tom. You got me." I use all the emotional power I can muster to keep from crying again.

He smiles and nods.

"I really need to use the bathroom. I've been holding it since I got here." We release our hands.

"Don't piss your pants for Christ's sake. Go." He waves me off.

"I'll be right back."

I leave the room and pass Shantelle in the hallway.

"You leaving?" Shantelle asks.

"Just using the bathroom, but shortly. I've got a few errands to run but I'd like to come back this evening. Maybe for dinner?"

"Okay. He don't eat much, but if you bring him a chocolate malt, he'll love you forever."

"I'll do that. Thanks. I'll say goodbye after I'm done using the bathroom."

"Okay honey."

I enter the hall bath and close the door behind me. The room hasn't changed a single iota, right down to the rugs and towels and brass shower door.

I pee, wash my hands, and take a look in the mirror. My eyes are red. I grab a tissue from the box sitting on the back of the toilet and blow my nose, tossing the tissue in the tiny white trash can next to the vanity when I finish.

Back at the mirror, I think about how happy I am that I don't wear mascara. The last time I stared into this mirror I was a pup, barely surviving with no idea where I was headed. Now, I'm a full-grown wolf, barely surviving with no idea where I'm headed. I know more but somehow still know nothing at all. That's a sad realization.

I see a flash of a woman behind me. I whip around and find nothing, but my heart races. I turn back to the mirror and look past my own reflection. The memory Dina managed to shake loose pops into my head. It's no wonder I'm always looking over my shoulder. Granted, there is the occupational hazard aspect to that, but I had no idea there was a deeper component to it that dates back to when my parents were killed. Will I ever have a day in my life where I can fully relax and let my guard down? If not, I fear the stress from that alone may kill me.

13

I said goodbye to Tom and assured him I'd come back this evening. He told me I'd better and that he had a surprise for me. I promised and left.

I'm sitting in my mini-van now, planning to go see an old hacker friend from my street-running Baltimore days that might be able to help me make a few anonymous phone calls. Not the dummy phone kind, but ones on VOIP through a VPN so I cannot be traced through cell towers, just in case the people I want to call are being tapped. Making a call from one dummy phone to another is one thing. Calling someone who has a trackable line that might be compromised is another. I can't take a risk and see the Leer family in-person but I will try to call them if my friend can set me up. I also plan to check in on a few other people too. Once I'm done with Baltimore, which will have to be sooner than later, it may be years before I can get back here, or I might not ever get back because it's entirely possible I'll be dead. Either way, I feel a strong desire to tie up any loose ends.

Finding Hakeem Miller might not be the easiest thing. He may not even be around here anymore. I know where he used to be and I know a few other places to look. He's like me. He lives in the underbelly of society, away from the prying eyes of big brother and the criminal justice system. I only hope there hasn't been a ton of change around here.

I went for a swim at the hotel before showing up to this part of town. At 2:30 in the afternoon, it's going to be a pain in the ass to find Hakeem. Business hours for the underground folks usually don't start before nine at night. On the plus side, there should be less thugs around for me to maneuver past.

The first location I decide to try is an old warehouse that was converted to apartments in the seventies. In all the years since then, I've been told it wavered from respectable housing for the poor to the now beat down, heavily graffitied, cash only housing of societal off-casts. Hakeem used to reside on the third floor. In the past, I only had to follow the black networking cables stapled to the ceiling of the third-floor hallway to find his place. So that's where I'll start.

The building, not surprisingly, has buzz-in or keyed entry. I pull the ol' wait until someone leaves and sneak in right before the door slams shut. Even at this time of day, I only had to wait ten minutes.

The first thing I notice upon on entry is the heat. No air conditioning. There might be window units in the apartments but the common areas have none. The second smack in the face is the odor. There are hints of cigar smoke, bacon grease, and the unwashed armpits of a fat guy that has no idea what deodorant is. I feel like I'm describing the notes of a good bottle of wine, except my head is inside the bowl of a truck stop bathroom toilet.

I do my best to ignore it and head up the stairs directly to the right. There's no elevator in a building like this. Well, there was an elevator. My guess is that it's now a makeshift garbage chute. I jog up the steps as not to wallow in the stench.

When I reach the second-floor platform, I pause a moment to let a guy coming down the stairs pass me. Of course, he doesn't just pass me. In this part of town, especially in a building like this, I'm giving off the 'I don't belong here, please stop and fuck with me' vibe.

The guy is about a head taller than me, thin, frazzled and dirty blonde hair. I'm pretty sure he's had meth in last 24 hours. He stops right in front of me, turns only his head, looks me up and down.

"You need some help baby?"

"Sure don't."

I move to walk past him and continue up the stairs but I'm forced to stop when he grabs my left arm at the elbow. Big mistake.

I yank free from his weak-ass grip and with my right arm out in front of my chest, I bull rush him, pushing and pinning him against the wall.

"Never fuckin' touch me. Ever."

He tries to squirm free but is powerless.

"Jesus ... you bitch."

Fuck this guy. I don't even think about how it might end up. I release my hold of him and with both hands grab his upper arms and just toss him down the stairs. His feet completely leave the floor and he travels in the air until he lands painfully on the landing below. His shoulders and upper back slam hard against the wall.

He cries out in pain but says nothing before switching to a continuous and staccato whimper.

I probably shouldn't have done that. I don't need the extra attention. I shake my head and leave him be, finally heading to the third floor where I finally make it to apartment 808. The actual number is 308 but someone used a permanent marker to change the three to an eight. I reach into my zip-up hoodie and click off the safety of the piece hanging under my left arm. When I knock on this door, there's no telling who might answer, so I need to be able react as fast as possible to defend myself. I don't see any bullet holes around so I'm at least going to assume it's not a shoot first policy.

I rap three times, hard, then take a big step back. At first, I don't hear anything. Suddenly, there's the screech of a wood chair across the floor, a shuffling of feet, and hard steps toward the door. The deadbolt clicks and a three-inch gap appears. A sliver of Hakeem's face instantly fills the space.

"What?" Hakeem barks.

He doesn't recognize me. I'm almost insulted.

"I was told you were the person to see if someone needs a little help with their computer."

"I don't do that anymore. Fuck off!"

He starts to slam the door but I interrupt with a firm, flat hand.

"I can't believe you don't remember me, Hakeem. It hasn't been that long."

He cocks his head and looks me over.

"It's me ... Josey, you fuckin' idiot. I hope you're not doing any of the meth that seems to be floating around in the air out here."

I release my hand from the door and it closes. The chain drags.

Hakeem opens the door and smiles.

"Josey Fuckin' Baldwin! Holy shit. Where the hell have you been? Get in here." He steps aside and I walk past him. The apartment is studio-style. There is a dining area and a kitchen to the right with a bathroom at the back. To the left, there is a large room that Hakeem has set up as a bedroom at the rear and a living room nearest the front door. And when I say living room, I mean there is a couch, a coffee table littered with computer gear, and in the place where a TV or entertainment center might be, there are six monitors mounted on the wall, three across and two down. It's impressive.

Hakeem closes the door and uses all the locks.

"My god," Hakeem says. "I wasn't sure I'd ever see your face again. You kind of vanished. Go ahead, take a seat. It's your hair that threw me off. I've never seen you blonde."

I walk over to the couch and sit on the end closest to the kitchen. The place is orderly and clean. I don't know why I'm surprised. Hakeem's always been this way. There's paint chipping on the ceiling, and the walls and the furniture are certainly out of date. Granted, there's no trash around, no scattered clothes, no pizza boxes. I guarantee you this apartment is the most well-kept one in the building.

"You know how it is. Hiding from people sometimes requires a physical change."

"Can I get you a drink?" He goes to the fridge, opens it, and peers inside. "Fuck, I don't have much. I could make a screwdriver or a rum and coke. I'm out of bottled water. Can't drink the shit from this faucet."

"I'm actually fine. Thanks for offering."

"I remember you could drink me under the table guuuurrrl." He shuts the fridge and leaves the kitchen.

"I drink brandy or scotch mostly, but rarely anymore. Can't afford to be impaired."

"Well, Miss Uppity. Only people that drink scotch are some old, rich white dudes. You an old, rich white dude now?" He joins me on the couch, sitting on the opposite end.

"The last time I checked, I'm still Josey Baldwin, although, I've moved up a little, I guess. Well, I did. I'm running now. That's kind of why I'm here. I need your help."

"What else is new? Only time anyone visits is when they need something." He gives me a scowl but quickly turns it into a smile.

"I know. I'm sorry. Trust me, it's better I don't see people too often. They'd probably end up dead."

"What kind of shit you into these days? And thank you for coming here to get me involved. I'm not fucked, am I?"

"Uhhh." I rub my forehead. "That's a long story, maybe for another time. Five cent version, I started working for an organization a few years ago and now I'm on the run from them. I need to make a few personal phone calls, no business shit, but I'm worried the people I need to call are being watched and I can't give up my location or they'd find me in a heartbeat."

"Sounds like you need a global VOIP relay. I can do that."

"I got money."

"For you, that won't be necessary."

"I insist. The risk for you is high enough that this favor has a price."

"Okay," he relents. "Let me get us setup." He grabs a keyboard and mouse combo pad from his coffee table and with the press of a key brings to life his wall of monitors. "Any details you can share about your predicament that won't get me killed? You mentioned earlier you worked for an organization. That sounds quite contrary to the lone-wolf Josey I used to know."

"Yeah. While it has provided some interesting opportunities for me, it's turning out to be more of a headache than I could've ever imagined. One big thing is finding out a lot about my past."

"How so? You say that like you're fifty years old."

"You know I was a foster kid. I never knew who my real parents were. I sure as hell know now. And the whole situation is fuckin' ugly." I let out a big exhale, shake my head. "I don't think I can even get into it right now without it messing me up."

"I understand." Hakeem lightly pats the space just above my knee. "Family stuff is always jacked. I'm about ready if you are."

"I'm ready."

"Look at the lower left screen. You see that box in the middle? That's where you put the phone number you want to call. Then press enter." He rises from the couch and finds a wireless headset on the underside of the coffee table. He turns it on, makes sure it's activated, and then hands it to me. "Put this on."

I place the headset on and then he puts the keyboard and mouse pad in my lap.

"Once you hit ENTER, the call will engage. Some buttons will appear on the screen after that. One is HOLD, the other is END CALL. Any questions?"

"Sounds easy enough."

"I'll step out for a bit. How much time you think you need?"

"Not more than thirty minutes."

"Okay. Can I get you a sandwich or something?"

"No thanks."

Hakeem goes to the kitchen, takes his cell phone, keys, and wallet from the counter, and goes to the front door to leave. After unlocking the door, he turns back to me. "Do not answer the door, no matter what."

"I won't. And, if you see a methed-out dickhead on the stairs that looks like he got his ass whooped, that was my handy work. He put his hands on me but he'll be fine."

"You were always a punch first kind of women. Respect."

"Can't afford not to."

He waves me on and leaves without saying another word.

With the keyboard on my legs, I type in the first number and hit ENTER.

I get Gabby's cell phone message greeting and the beep. I debate for one second whether to hang up or not, but I stay on.

"Hey, Gabby. It's Josey. I know it's been awhile. I've had no way to contact you before now and I wish I could see you guys in-person but that's not possible. I miss you guys. Maybe someday we'll get to see each other again but it may not be for a longtime. Just know I'm always thinking of you guys. I'm going to send you a care package via UPS. Be looking for it. Love you all."

I end the call.

I hate that my life has become so complicated that I don't dare even do a late-night visit. By the time I get to see them again, I might not recognize Evie. They'll appreciate the package. I'm going to put ten-grand in a box with a bunch of bags of sour gummies and send it out tomorrow. I guarantee they can use the money. And what kid doesn't like sour candy? Only the pain-in-the-ass ones, if you ask me.

While I have a chance, I'm going to call a few ladies I want to check in on, just to make sure they aren't being harassed. Before joining AWT, I had assisted several women in escaping an assault or some much worse situation. Afraid to even date women knowing that I might be watching, most of these men that I reeducated eventually left the greater Baltimore area. Regardless, I want to make sure. If there are any issues I can correct while I'm here, I will. Beyond that, I will no longer be involved.

Forty-three minutes after leaving, Hakeem returns, using his keys to get in. I reflexively had my hand on one of my guns until I saw his face and was certain he was alone.

I stand up.

Hakeem heads straight to the kitchen with a white paper sack and a tan plastic grocery bag. He empties the bags out onto the counter. There are two orders of fries, four sandwiches, two bottles of water, a 20-ounce diet 7-up, a 20-ounce regular 7-up, and an assortment of napkins, seasoning packets, and dipping sauces.

"Help yourself," he says. "There's enough for both of us if you want any."

The smell of the food is hard to resist. I go over, seize a bottle of water and one of the orders of fries.

"What kind of sandwiches you got there?"

"Two are cheeseburgers, one is a grilled chicken, the other a crispy chicken. Take your pick. I'll eat whatever."

"Thank you." I grab the thickest one, which I assume is one of the burgers. I guessed right. I take down a handful of fries, then unfurl the burger wrapping. "I'm hungrier than I thought."

"No prob. Calls go okay?"

"Yeah. Perfect. That was a big help." I stop stuffing my face and use a napkin to wipe my fingers. From my left cargo pants thigh pocket, I pull five, one-hundred dollar bills out and slide them over to Hakeem. "Here. And don't dare argue with me over it. The favor is bigger than you know."

He sighs, takes a sip of his soda. "Fine." He doesn't bother to take the money yet. "So, you gonna give me any clue what you're up to?"

"The less you know, the more plausible deniability you'll have."

"Come on now. I'm not some bitch ass mutha-fucka from the westside. I can handle myself."

"With all due respect, these people are not like any of the assholes we're used to dealing with around here. They take privacy and secrecy as seriously as anything and will not hesitate to end you to keep their secrets. You'll just have to trust me when I say that."

"I believe it. You said you're on the run from them. How do you ever hope to get away?"

"Not quite sure yet. I'll just keep moving around for now. There are a few things going on within the company that might pan out in my favor, but then again, they might not. Most likely, I'll end up overseas somewhere, although, that's no guarantee of anything. Their reach is without limit."

"Good luck, Josey. Sincerely. If there is anything else I can do to help, just let me know."

"I will. Thanks. Don't wait by the phone." I smile.

We finish eating with little else to say aside from the groans of pure cheeseburger satisfaction.

I use the bathroom but don't dare look in the mirror. It's getting to the point where I just want to smash the damn things when I see them. Fuck mirrors. Fuck Madame K.

I return to the living room. "I gotta get outta here. Thanks again. I was never here."

Hakeem gives me a long hug before I leave. "Be safe and don't take shit from no one."

"I'll do my best."

I walk out and leave the building without incident. My new meth friend is nowhere to be found.

I'm exhausted and need a nap before I go back to visit Tom, so I head to my hotel to do just that. Despite the fact

I'm worried about damn near everything, I know once I hit that bed, I'll be out.

14

I stop by a local ice cream shack on my way back to see Tom. They have these amazing dinner plate size tenderloins, so I get a few of those, some tater tots, and one each of chocolate, vanilla, and strawberry shakes. I figure I'll let Tom have his choice, then the nurse and I can fight over what's left.

I park a little closer this time, just four houses down, and walk with hurried steps. In this mid-August heat, the shakes are already melting.

Shantelle answers the door without saying a word. She appears somber and is less talkative then before. She follows me to the kitchen where I place the food and drinks down on the counter.

"I got some sandwiches and tots." I pull the food out of the bag. "I didn't know what flavor to get Tom for his shake, so I got the three basics. The rest is for you and me to share, if you want any." I look to Shantelle. Her facial expression sends a chill up the back of my neck.

"Honey, there's no good way to say this, but Tom just

passed away, like less than five minutes ago. Medical is on their way now."

"Wait. What? I don't," I try to finish my thought but the words don't form. I shake my head. "What happened?"

"It was peaceful. He was napping and he just didn't wake up. I'm really sorry."

I put my right hand over my mouth. My mind goes blank. I close my eyes. My breath is shallow."

"Do you want to sit down?"

I hear Shantelle speak but it's like she's in a tunnel some hundred feet away from me. She comes around and puts one hand on my back, one at my elbow.

I shake my head and open my eyes. I fully expect to bust out crying but for some reason I don't.

"If you're feeling up to it, you should go in and see him, say goodbye. There's not going to be a visitation or a funeral. Might not get another chance."

I nod. "Okay."

"Take your time. I won't send in the medic until after you come out."

I nod again and leave the kitchen.

When I reach the partially ajar bedroom door, I place my hand on the knob, hesitating for a few seconds to push it open. I don't know why I'm scared. I've seen all manner of dead bodies, from exploded ones to bullet riddled one to the bloated from floating down the river for two days kind. I guess it's not the body I'm afraid of but the fact that when I enter this room, I'll be doing so for the last time. Having just said my final goodbyes to Dina, I don't know how ready I am to do it again, especially with someone I care deeply about.

I push open the door and take one step in, analyzing the scene before me. The stillness bothers me. Tom is on the bed, positioned just as he was when I left earlier today. The sheet and blanket are up to his neck. His head is tilted slightly toward me. I half expect his eyes to open. They don't, of course, but goddamn it I wish they would.

I step over to the end of the bed but no closer. I can't bear to touch him. I can only think of one thing to say.

"Thank you. Thank you. Thank you."

My eyes tear up but I manage to hold back a full-on outburst.

"I'm glad I got to know you Sake Tom. I do hope you get to see your wife again. And if I'm lucky, we'll meet again too."

I look to the ceiling and shake my head. A memory pops into my head, a time of significant impact on my development.

"Ouch! That fuckin' hurt." I shook my hand.

Tom kept pressing me to stay on guard. We'd been sparring with Bo staves, well, really, they were just two mop handles from Tom's old restaurant, but close enough.

"You're lazy," Tom said.

"No, I'm not. I'm tired."

"Ooohhh, you're tired," Tom mocked. "You think your enemy gives a crap that you're tired?"

He swung at me but missed as I backed up a few feet. We started circling.

"I don't have any enemies."

"But you will. You're a smart-ass and a woman. Everyone will be your enemy."

Clearly, he was just trying to piss me off. I launched an overhead strike, coming down hard on his staff. He smiled but was able to push me away with ease. I stepped back again and the dance continued.

"Right now, *you're* my enemy," I said as I started swinging wildly in front of him, making no contact.

"Yes, I am, so you shouldn't believe a word I say." He threw his staff aside. "Now hit me."

I was confused. I had no idea what to do. I didn't think he was trying to trick me, but maybe that was the test.

He didn't say anything else, just stared back, revealing nothing to me.

I wanted to engage, the fire in my belly telling me to

charge, but as I listened closely to my instincts, I could hear them telling me to quit.

I threw down my staff.

Tom smiled and nodded. "Well done."

"Another lesson?"

"Always. You must be prepared to defend yourself, but you must also know when enough is enough. If you look into the eyes of your enemy and suddenly you see their humanity, you must match them in kind or you'll become them."

"That sounds a little movie quote. How do you come up with this shit?"

"I've watched a lot of Japanese samurai movies from the sixties and seventies, so, yeah. Doesn't mean I'm not right. Clean up." He started walking toward the house. "I'll make some tea and a snack. Bring the mop handles."

I'm not sure why that memory came forward as I stand here over my friend's lifeless body. Back then, in that moment, I was so pissed off. My hands hurt like a son of a bitch and he just kept saying shit to aggravate me. But he was right. Everyone is my enemy, but while I fight against the world, I have to be careful not to lose my humanity. It didn't really sink in much at the time, yet somehow, I've managed to live it. I think I do, anyway. I'm here visiting my friend and mentor, even in the midst of my own personal crisis, so yeah, I'm definitely trying.

I leave the room and return to the kitchen. Shantelle is munching on some tater tots, dipping each one in ketchup.

I join in, taking sips of the strawberry shake between every few bites of the tenderloin. I'm not really all that hungry. I could just be stress eating. There's a comfortable and needed silence between us as we eat. She's been in these situations many times before. It's obvious. She understands the temperature of the room she's in and acts accordingly. A true professional and a welcome one.

The medic from the coroner's office arrives a few minutes later. I decide to step outside for some air while the woman and Shantelle take care of this end of the ordeal.

I'm working hard to keep myself from funneling down a depression spiral. All I can think about is getting back to my room at the hotel and downing just enough scotch to get me stupid but not quite enough to make me puke.

As I sit on the steps, I lose all track of time as my mind wanders from one disjointed thought to another. I go from moments where I want to rip out my hair to ones where I want to jump up and just start running with no destination in mind. When I settle down, I close my eyes and all I see is Tom in that damn medical bed, silent, still. It's breaking me down in ways I would've never expected.

The coroner leaves the house, passing me on the stairs, and just in time to shake me momentarily from the pain. I decide to go back in to at least say goodbye and thank you to Shantelle.

She greets me in the living room. She has a large manila envelope in her hand.

"This is for you. He gave it to me a few hours after you left this morning." She hands it to me. "He told me to tell you not to open it here. Wait until you're alone somewhere."

"Umm ... okay. I wanted to ask. His arrangements, are they all taken care of, like paid for and everything?"

"Oh yes. He prearranged and prepaid. He's to be cremated, placed in a special urn and buried with his wife. There won't be any services of any kind. His wishes. He told me that anyone he ever knew that might have come to his funeral are probably all dead now, save for you."

"What about his stuff and the house?"

"He said it was all taken care of. He hired an attorney to handle the estate. If I remember correctly, he said a company would come in and auction off his belongings and then sell the house. That's all I know."

"Thank you, by the way, for taking care of him. I know you're doing a job, but I can tell you really care. So, thank you."

"I 'preciate that. He sure was fond of you. I'm just glad

you came by when you did. Fortunate for you both."

"You know what, I just realized I don't have any pictures of him. I don't think I ever took a single shot of him back in the day. That sucks."

I look around the room and spot a five by seven framed picture on the coffee table that I remember noticing earlier.

"I know it might not be appropriate, but do you think it'd be okay if I took that photo on the coffee table of Tom and his wife? I can imagine all of his personal items will just get thrown away anyway."

"You're the only person who even came to visit him. You take that photo and don't even worry about it."

"Great. Thanks." I go over and grab it from the table. It looks like it was taken while they were on a vacation many years ago, probably long before I was born. And they looked as happy as two people could be. It makes my heart swell.

"So, what happens now with his body?"

"The place doing the cremation will be by soon to take him away. Then my part's done. You can stick around if you like."

"I'd rather not, honestly. I would like to go downstairs for just a moment. When I lived here, that's where my room was."

"He mentioned that. Said there's nothing down there now. Flooded real bad two years ago so he took everything out of there. Now it's just an old, wet, stinky basement."

"Well, it was an old, wet, stinky basement then too. But it was better than being homeless."

"Go ahead if you want to. Just be careful on those steps."

"I will. Won't be but a minute."

I place the picture and the envelope down on the table and make my way to the basement door, through the kitchen near the back of the house. I open it and flick the light switch. I take each step one at a time to ensure they won't collapse under me. I glance around to discover that not even the disgusting bathroom or paneled walls remain. Now there's nothing but cinder block walls, crumbling concrete floors, and dirt. That's enough of this shit.

I return to the living room, grab my stuff from the table, and head to the front door.

"I'm gonna take off. Thanks again for everything."

"You wanna take any of that food with ya?"

"You can keep it or pitch it."

"Okay then. Good luck to ya. My condolences for Tom."

I smile and nod. I leave the house, get to my car, and drive away, heading to nowhere. I just keep moving around the greater Baltimore area until an hour passes. Eventually, I notice the sun is getting close to the horizon, so I take a detour and head toward the bay where I used to sit on the docks and think.

The briny air is a calming reminder of a time in my life when things were simpler. It also fucks me up a bit when little Evie comes to mind. My life was far from perfect or safe back then but at least I could see the Leers from time to time. Doing so now might get them killed and almost certainly get me found.

I walk all the way down to the far southern docks and then to a small platform where the water is only a foot from the top. There's no one else around and I have Tom's envelope in hand.

I take a seat on the edge of the boardwalk, remove my shoes and socks, and dip my feet in. The cool water gives me a little charge but I adjust quickly. I kick and splash a little as I stare out across the bay, the sun casting the last of its light from my left and out into the bay. The smattering of low-level clouds offers an even more beautiful array of colors and shapes.

It was Tom who taught me to appreciate a good sunset, something I barely paid attention to in my youth. *The world is full of darkness and hate and anger,* he once told me, *but it also has beauty and love and hope. If you don't stop once in a while to appreciate those amazing things, you'll get lost in the bad. Don't get lost there. It's a terrible trap.*

His words have me thinking about what the rest of my life

might hold and how I want to proceed with the situation I currently find myself in. If only there was a place I could go and just start over, where no one knows me, where no one would ever think to look for me, not ever.

Curiosity grabs at me as I cling to the envelope from Tom, so I pinch the metal prongs and open it. I peek inside to find a few pieces of paper. I remove them and notice one feels heavier than it should. I separate the last sheet from the rest and discover there is no writing on it but there is what looks like a standard house key taped to the middle of the page. I put that page back in the envelope and place it under my right thigh.

The other three sheets of paper are written in pen and read as follows:

Dear Josey,

If you're reading this it means I've passed to the great unknown. I won't bore you with any more words of wisdom. I'm sure you tired of my shit years ago and stopped listening anyway. And you should have. I'm an old man that talked too much and you were too nice to tell me to shut the hell up. And I don't want you crying or depressed over me either. I lived a long time, maybe too long. I only hope to see Fumi again.

The truth is, despite the fact that we've only known each other a few short years, you were the closest thing I ever had to a daughter. I've never told anyone this, but that was the one thing I could never give Fumi as I've been sterile my entire adult life. She never made a fuss over it but I know deep down it bothered her not to have children. We had thought many times about adoption, but with all the hours we worked running the restaurant, we just never found the time.

And let me tell you, she would have loved you even more than I do. You are just like her. Fiery, independent, and a survivor. Keep being those and you'll be just fine.

I'm sorry if I was ever too hard on you, but for some reason I knew you could handle it, and more importantly, you needed it. Some of us need to be pushed, and pushed hard to get on the right path. I was like that too, and I saw in you that same thing.

My shitty house and all my shitty things will be auctioned off and the money given to a local children's hospital, after the bloodsucking lawyer takes his cut.

Another thing that no one else knows is that I have a cabin retreat in the mountains of South Carolina. It's in a trust that now belongs to you. Your actual name isn't on it anywhere, so it cannot be traced back to you. That key is for the front door. I've also included a detailed map of its location. It's a nice little place on a couple of acres with a little creek running behind it. I was always paranoid of banks and the scumbags of wall street, so I frequently took bundles of cash up there and hid them in the return air registers. That money is now yours as well. I lost track of how much there is years ago, but if I had to guess, I wouldn't be surprised if there was four or five hundred thousand by now.

I'm so glad you came to see me again. I thought about you often and missed you more than I care to admit. I hope you can find some kind of peace and happiness. You've never shared much of an interest in doing so, but I would suggest you go find a nice man and have lots of kids. It'll calm you right the hell down and give you something to care about more than you will ever care about yourself. I might be joking here, but then again, I might not be.

With all the sincerity of my heart and soul,
Sake Tom

I close my eyes and hold the pages to my chest, my hands trembling. I'm still not sure what the hell just happened. I've been back in Baltimore for like a minute and my friend Tom is dead and it's been suggested to me that I have kids. I'm trying not to be glib in light of my friend's death, but I think I may have landed in an alternate dimension.

I'm seriously thinking of jumping in the bay and just swimming out until I can't move my arms and legs anymore, finally stopping to let my body sink into the water and down to the bottom. I won't, of course, but the idea of getting away from this mess still rings true. I do have this piece of paper with a key attached. If I somehow managed to get to this cabin, unbeknownst to the company, would I really have a chance to reboot my life or would this just be a temporary reprieve? I think I owe it to myself to try. Yes. I do. I will.

I need to get out of this city and now I know where I'm going. How long will it last? I'll try to stay optimistic, despite my nature. I wish I could go see Vick before I go, and the Leers. Unfortunately, if I'm going to start over, I have to leave this all behind. I need to call Ollie to get an update and then I'm out. I don't want to be surrounded by death anymore. I don't want to sleep with one eye open anymore. I don't want to think about any of this anymore, not for one more second.

15

At AWT

In a conference room on the top floor, across the building from Madame K's office, the entire leadership group of AWT sits around a massive table awaiting their boss and the emergency meeting she called for.

Of the eight chairs, there are three empty seats at the round table. Clockwise from there are Li Xia, Greg Mantz, Benjamin Nazarian, and Ollie Washington.

Jessica Noel, secretary and assistant to Madame K, enters the room first, followed by her boss. Jessica steps aside and allows Madame K to pass, then she makes sure the door is shut and takes her seat to Madame K's left. The one empty seat is a painful reminder of Dina. They all feel it.

"I'd like to start off by acknowledging how much Dina will be missed at this company," Madame K says. "I don't have much else to say about that, other than I'm currently working on her replacement. I should have some information on that front in the next month or so."

Jessica is furiously taking notes on her tablet as Madame K speaks.

"The main reason I called you all here is to discuss the

matter of Josey Baldwin, and even more importantly, this pervasive notion that it might be time for me to step down from the leadership of this company, a company I helped create. Since the topics of Miss Baldwin and this damn mutiny are clearly tied together, I'll address both. Before I get started, does anyone have anything to say?"

Madame K looks around the room, stopping momentarily at each person for signs of wanting to speak. The room stays silent.

"Good. Twenty-five years ago, long before any of you were around, and a few years before this company was really even the thing it is today, I accepted a contract in a small town outside of Pittsburgh. A husband and wife that worked for a local mining company. Whistleblower type deal. We generally don't accept those kinds of contracts now, I know, but back then, there were no rules, no pesky little scruples, and certainly no fuckin' feelings. It was a different world.

"At the time, a little consortium had formed. There were four of us then, and it morphed into AWT. There had been discussions about how we'd go about recruiting people to work for us, and one of the ideas I floated, one that was quickly dismissed, was targeting young, at-risk youth to form and mold into future assassins. That was when the stupid idea emerged that there would be lines we wouldn't cross, but I disagreed."

Everyone was really paying attention now. They're all fixated on Madame K, taking in the details of what they hope will be answers to questions all of them have been asking for some time. What Madame K hopes to accomplish with her narrative remains to be seen.

"During the execution of the aforementioned contract, I came across the couple's daughter in the bathroom. Protocol insisted I leave no witnesses, no exceptions, but when I saw that little girl's reflection in the mirror and she saw me, I could see in her eyes that she understood what had happened, yet she didn't cry or scream. In that moment, my recruitment plan popped into my head, and with no thought for the dirty details, I decided to let that girl live."

Everyone's eyes go big. Ollie rubs his chin and wants to speak but he keeps it in. The rest of the room is still and attentive, maybe even afraid to move. No one dare.

"And yes, I know, that is unacceptable behavior, but I had an idea I wanted to explore so I made a rash decision. I took the little girl and placed her with a woman that ran a children's home outside of Baltimore. My hope was that I would figure out a way to raise the girl, train her, and who knows what. I may have even had this grandiose idea of making her into my future successor. I wasn't really sure.

"Truth is, after some months, I just couldn't find the time or the will to go through with my hazy plans, having been convinced by the others that children were off limits. So, I abandoned the idea, and ultimately, that meant abandoning Josey as well."

Ollie raises his right hand like a student wanting to ask a question but not wanting to interrupt.

"Go ahead," Madame K says.

"With all due respect, why in the hell did you allow her into the Kill Academy knowing all this, or at the very least, why didn't you tell us the truth about it upfront?"

"I should have been upfront about her, but as you might recall, I did give some resistance to bringing her in."

"Yeah, well, I remember we kind of went back and forth on that. At first, you insisted we try to recruit her, then later you got flaky on it, but then ultimately you insisted on rigging a mission to make sure she succeeded. This whole thing is utterly confusing, and quite frankly, starting to sound like a load of bullshit."

"Fair enough. I don't deny, then and now, I made some choices that turned out to be less than ideal. I can even understand the distrust many of you may have now, but I assure you, I've learned a valuable lesson about trust, and going forward, I plan to be more inclusive and upfront with all of you. We have a good thing going here, and I'm not quite ready to give up on it. I hope you all feel the same and can come around."

As ballsy as ever, Li Xia speaks up. "And if we don't?"

Madame K tilts her head a bit to one side, takes a deep breath, exhales. "I'd really rather not entertain that option. Here is what I will do. After this meeting, each one of you may choose to leave or stay, with no strings attached. I'd like the opportunity to continue leading all of you, with a new focus on trust and transparency. That won't be easy. I understand that, fully. But as you've done in the past, I'm asking that we find our common origins and reboot to that time and place in an effort to fix our current issues."

"I find it hard to grasp," Ollie says before rubbing his chin and continuing, "that any one of us can just walk out of here with no consequences. This world we operate in rarely affords an opportunity like that."

"To put this plainly, I simply don't want a bad outcome here, for me or for any of you."

"Tell that to Ridge," Ollie snips.

"That," Madame K puts up her left index finger, "was about abject failure, not about leaving or staying. But let's get back on track here. I want all of you to continue working here. I want to continue here as well, at least for a time. I realize I'm on the tail end of my tenure. I hope to do so with all of you by my side."

There is now a silence in the room. It lasts a full minute. Each person ponders their place at AWT, their options for the future, the true risk of leaving or staying. In the world of assassins, there are always degrees of difficulty, and therein lies the complicated nature of the decision they must all make.

"Does anyone else have any questions or doubts? Now would be the time, because once you leave this room, it will either be as an AWT asset or as a former one."

Finally, Greg Mantz speaks up. "Any chance we can take a few days to think about it?" There are few nods around the table.

"I'm afraid that won't be possible. There is urgent work to

do and in order to keep this company from falling apart completely, I feel it would be best to reboot immediately."

"I'm only going to say this as someone playing devil's advocate here," Benjamin Nazir says, "definitely not my personal opinion."

"Go ahead," Madame K encourages.

"We essentially heard two options. As individuals, we can stay or we can go. Obviously, there has been this undercurrent of you, personally, leaving. Are you willing to entertain that possibility? Amicably, of course, let's say, if a vote was taken and everyone agreed that was the best option?"

"Thank you for your direct question. I appreciate your willingness to be so forthcoming. As your leader, I acknowledge that has not always been so easy to do with me, and I look forward to improving in that area. But to answer your question, I am not presenting that as an option and here's why. I would much rather go out on a positive note than as part of a mutiny. I think I deserve that much. Am I perfect? No. Are there things I would have done differently? Yes. But I'm sure this is true of all of us. I can clearly see the end of the road for me in this business. I simply want the opportunity to correct my wrongs and leave, in short order, under better circumstances."

"And what about Josey?" Ollie asks.

"I'm sure most or all of you would like me to just let her go, but I will never feel comfortable knowing she's out there with the knowledge she has, and very likely, a strong urge to kill me. If you stay on, we will pursue her and do what must be done. At this point, there is no rectifying the situation with her, so her fate has been decided. Anything else?"

There are a few quick glances around, some barely noticeable shrugging shoulders, but otherwise, no one else speaks up.

"Great. By a show of hands, which of you are staying? Remember, this is a one-time offer, good only right now, with no repercussions should any of you decide to leave."

Madame K looks around the table for raised hands or any inclination thereof. One by one, each person sitting at the table, aside from Madame K herself and Jessica, raises a hand in a unanimous show of support.

A smile, albeit brief, sneaks across Madame K's face. She nods in acceptance of the better than expected result of the meeting.

"I'm happy this has turned out to be a positive experience. I hope we can continue on this new path." Madame K rises from her chair. "I also hope to have private discussions with all of you soon. For now, we'll be diverting some resources to the pursuit of Josey Baldwin. I want her found and I want her dead. Meeting adjourned. Consider that an official kill order."

Madame K leaves the room, Jessica in tow.

Once the door shuts behind them, a collective sigh of relief can be felt as the oxygen returns to the room.

"I guess we have our orders," Ollie says.

No one dare have an in-depth discussion at AWT for fear of being heard by any known or unknown surveillance. Those conversations will be had at a later time.

For now, they each leave the room and scatter to their respective offices, no doubt, to process the meeting's revelations. And although they each agreed to stay on and support Madame K for the time being, respect and trust are not renewed so easily.

16

I'm still a bit numb after Tom's death. After getting in late last night, I laid in my hotel bed, staring at the ceiling, kind of zoned out, finally falling asleep after a few hours that seemed like days.

I woke up this morning with a fog of anger restricting my thoughts and mind. I got on the road before nine on my way to this cabin I inherited from Tom. I'm not sure what I expect to find there. Hopefully my sanity will appear.

I'll be on the road for about eight hours before getting there. I'm nearly half-way there at this moment and ready for a snack break.

I pull off the freeway in a small town with a Best Western hotel, a McDonald's, and a gas station with an attached Arby's. I could go for a roast beef and some curly fries.

At pump number eight, I fill up with gas and pay inside. I return to my car and go through the Arby's drive-through. I choose a spot facing the street and park to eat. My bites are slow as I contemplate my life since first being approached by Dina to join the Kill Academy. I haven't had much time to fully analyze the decision Madame K made to keep me alive after killing my parents.

The protocol we assassins live and die by is that there can

be no witnesses, period. Even the sharp-edged Madame K would dispatch a witness with no hesitation, even a child, from the stories I've heard. Why she chose not to kill me at that moment is a baffling question. Even more confusing is her continued involvement thereafter. She went through all the trouble of taking me away from the house, keeping the dead bodies of my parents from my sight, then securing me a place within a children's home where it appears to have been rigged to make sure I would never be adopted, nearly ensuring I would end up a street rat. Just the kind of hard-edged person she might someday recruit.

Is that what this is really all about? Building the next generation of recruits? That can't be it because it doesn't make much sense. I could have just as easily been a model child and student, one that obeyed the rules, got good grades and went to college, excelled in life. She had no way of knowing what I'd become.

There were many ways that Rosemary made my life difficult, no question, but there were just as many ways in which I made life difficult with my own behavior and attitude. I'm naturally averse to authority and I anger easily. In the environment of a children's home, under the direction of someone like Rosemary Greenburg, there was no chance for that to end well. But again, Madame K had no idea that would be the case.

Regardless, I feel raw about what happened to my parents and I want some sort of vengeance. That's rather stupid and ironic, I know, considering my profession as a contract killer. The thing is, I would fully understand if someone wanted to take me out for killing their loved one. I would fight it because I want to be alive, but I would sure as hell understand the desire. And if they succeeded, more power to them. Maybe Ollie can clue me in.

I grab one of my dummy phones and call him.

He answers but doesn't speak.

"It's Josey."

"I know," Ollie answers. "I wasn't sure I'd ever hear from

you again."

"This might be the last time."

"Probably for the better."

I'm surprised by his curt and emotionless answer. "Well, Jesus, sorry I even bothered."

"I'm sorry, it's not that I didn't want to hear from you, it's just," Ollie hesitates.

"What? What's going on? Other than the usual."

"We had a big meeting with Madame K. The entire leadership group has agreed to stay on and let her stay too."

"Oh. I'm a little surprised but considering the risks, I totally get it. That's probably not good for me though, right?"

"Not exactly. She gave us the full explanation as to why you're alive and why she did what she did when you were young."

"I have a few ideas. Do tell."

"Basically, she had this crazy notion of very, very early recruitment techniques. You were to be an experiment for her on that front, but she gave up on the idea after a time, permanently abandoning you to the care of Dr. Greenburg."

"That's so weird. That very thought just crossed my mind, like we have ESP. Jesus. What are the odds I would still end up being recruited? That's the part that makes no sense. Obviously, she must have kept an eye on me."

"We're not one hundred percent sure if we were steered your way or not. Regardless, here we are and the news gets worse."

"Oh?"

"She's issued a kill order on you. I'm afraid you can never come back and you'll be hunted. I can put up some subtle roadblocks, as you still have allies here, but that may only go so far."

"Doesn't matter. I'm going away."

"I'm not sure that will make any difference. When AWT wants to find someone, they will, eventually."

"I understand. I'll try nonetheless. I wish it didn't have to be this way. If I thought I could confront Madame K without a high risk of my own death, I'd challenge her, but some self-preservation seems in order."

"I wish I could do more. But hey, since this might be our last conversation, I just wanted to say that I'm sorry you were brought into this mess. You did nothing to deserve this."

"Thanks. I know. I certainly don't blame *you*."

"Ya know, things change. If you last long enough, check in with me down the road. There could be some developments here at AWT. Nothing lasts forever."

"I wouldn't count on it. I need to leave all this bullshit behind. I do appreciate the sentiment."

There's a silence between us that lasts fifteen seconds.

"I don't know what else to say," Ollie says to break up the awkward empty space.

"I guess we'll just leave it at that then. Goodbye, Ollie."

I don't even wait for a response, ending the call.

In a few hours, I'll be at my new home, one I hope will spur a new direction for my life, one without constant death and fear and corruption. If there is one thing I am certain of, it's that I am resilient. A new place, a new name, and a whole new me. With time and a little luck, Annie will live a long, happily ever after.

Part II
My Present

17

Fall seems to have come early this year. We're not even out of September yet the weather has turned chilly and rainy, forcing the trees to prematurely begin their color change. As I cruise through the countryside to my new temporary home, a wash of tranquility flows over me. I don't know for sure if it's the setting, my resolve, or the anticipation for starting over that has me in such a peaceful state of mind, but whichever it is, it doesn't truly matter. The feeling is welcome.

Just as I start to find the limits of my driving time for the day, I spot the rural street sign marked 1250 E with a triple stemmed birch tree right behind, just like Tom's instructions stated.

I turn right and watch the miles on my odometer tick up two more. A few beats later, I see on the right a property with dozens of mature trees, shaded on the edges by their foliage, and nestled just in the center of them is a rustic, faded brown cabin with chipping paint and a mossed-over green roof. I can see mushrooms scattered on the ground in a few places, wildflowers and weeds in others.

I pull into what I believe is the driveway. It's only dirt but has the faint, worn remnants of tire indentations. I wonder how long it's been since Tom has visited this place. I suppose, depending on his health, it may have been a few years.

I park a few feet from the stone pathway that leads to the front door, turn off the car, and get out. With my head tilted back some, I close my eyes, taking in and releasing a few deep breaths. When I open them, I take a hard look at the cabin and instantly feel like this might be a mistake. Oh ... but that fresh air and the sounds of birds and insects. This place lacks all the noises and distractions of civilization, and that thought is all that keeps me from jumping back in the car to find an alternative.

I dig the front door key from my pants pocket and walk to the front porch. There's room enough to the right for a bistro set, if one were so inclined, but right now there are two plastic Adirondack chairs, that if I had to guess, were once white but are now varying shades of moss and mud.

I insert the key, turn the somewhat stiff lock, and push the door open with a twist of the knob. I half expect a pack of bats to fly past me but my imagination is funnier than real life. My instincts tell me to look for a light switch, but I know that won't do any good. Tom left me detailed instructions on the solar panel, propane tank, and generator situation. I'll have to go to town to see a guy at the hardware store to get the generator serviced and up and running. That will have to wait until tomorrow. For now, I pull a flashlight from my left pants pocket and twist the end.

I take a few steps in, shifting the beam of white LED light from corner to corner and across the floor in front of me. To the left is a small living room with a couch, a chair, two end tables with lamps, and a wood-burning fireplace. To the right is an even smaller space with an eat-in kitchen. The cabinets, card table and chairs, appliances, and living room furniture are antiquated and in desperate need of an upgrade, something I'll have to work on if I intend to stay here for any significant period of time. There are four doors in the room, in addition to the three windows. Next to the refrigerator is a door that leads back outside, and in front of me are two side by side doors.

I go to and open the one on the right first to discover the bathroom. It's not as dirty as I expected and perhaps the most newly remodeled of what I've seen so far, though still older than I'd like.

The second door reveals the lone bedroom. It's a tiny bit smaller than the living room but adequate. The only window is to the left. The queen bed is paired with nightstands, lamps, and a dresser on the opposite wall from the headboard. This is another space that is more up-to-date than the rest, much like the bathroom. I'll probably replace the mattress but leave the rest, assuming the furniture doesn't turn out to be more disgusting with the real lights on. I'll hopefully find that out tomorrow.

I walk to the kitchen door, which is half glass, and peek through. I can't see much past the dirt, but I do see an old charcoal grill and toward the back of the cabin, the generator.

I return to the front door with a list already forming in my head of the household items and cleaners I will need to purchase. Hopefully, the local hardware store where I need to get the generator serviced will have everything. They also have an IGA for groceries and a gas station to help pick up the slack. In a town of about seven hundred people, I'm lucky to have those. A web search also revealed a greasy spoon I can guarantee will have the best biscuits and gravy ever, and probably the weakest coffee that won't do at all. That's okay though. I'll get a Keurig machine anyway.

I suddenly remember there is money stashed in this place, at least that's what Tom told me. He had no reason to lie about it, and with his distrust of government, I'm not surprised that he would keep cash out of the system.

He told me there is air register on the wall of the kitchen that backs up to the bathroom, near the floor and just above the basemoulding. It's the only one in the entire cabin and doesn't belong. A house only needs air return if there is a forced air system, something this place lacks. The register is a clever façade.

I go over to the register and shine my light on it. Two flathead screws hold it in place. No problem. I bust out my trusty folding utility knife and use it to remove the screws. Sure enough, stacked in the cavity are bundles of money excessively wrapped in plastic. I pull two of them out. Two more drop down.

I cut the plastic off one and discover this bundle has ten-grand in it, all one hundred-dollar bills. Damn, Tom. You must have been some kind of hustler. I open the second one and get the same results. I'll wait until tomorrow to find out how much more is in there. I replace the register and grab the bundles to take with me.

For now, I think I'm done here. I'll back track to a bigger town to get a room for tonight then come back to the little town of Burton in the morning. I'll have a busy day of getting the generator running, shopping, and most importantly, cleaning the hell out of this place.

I head outside, locking the door behind me. On my way to the car, I glance over to my right and notice a shallow gully past the house. I walk over the spongey ground to the edge and find the gully is only about three feet deep. There is water at the bottom that might be eight to ten inches deep, gently flowing to my left. What a great find. I could sit here and just listen to this creek all day.

I get on the road going in the direction I originally came from. Having seen the property now, I feel at ease with being here and I hope I can build a life, at least for a while. Perhaps the remote nature of it will make it easier to move on. I do wonder how long it will be before Madame K finds me. I'm trying to stay positive on that front, hoping she never will. The realist in me says this will be a temporary stop.

Some part of me says just go ahead and show up on the doorstep of AWT and whatever happens, will happen. The problem is that I don't want to die. Despite the nature and danger of my life choices, I want to live and be safe. I just don't know any other way to live. Figuring out how to do that will be a challenge, no doubt, but will be essential if I intend to move on.

18

I arrive in Burton at 9:30 in the morning after a great night's sleep, perhaps the best I've had in months. Not a single person I know, and I don't know many, has a clue where the fuck I am. You can't buy that kind of peace.

I pull into an angled parking spot in front of the Farmer and Son's Hardware store. The building rests smack in the middle of the downtown area on the aptly named Main Street. It cuts right through town and anything of importance, outside of general housing, is in this little area. There is a little traffic but most of the cars driving by are just passing through on their way to somewhere else.

I look up and down the block to check out the architecture. The buildings seem to be in good shape, mostly clad in stone and brick, full of single pane windows. They're definitely old. I'm no expert but I'd say this town existed long before World War I.

I push open the hardware store's wood-framed, glass panel door. The bell above the door is crazy loud. Ain't no sneaking into this place. The space is filled floor to ceiling with a combination of wood and metal racks full of just about anything a local DIYer might need for their project. The lighting is from overhead long fluorescents which more than adequately brighten the space.

There's an older gentleman behind a long counter to my left. We make eye contact and exchange smiles.

"Hey there. Anything I can help you find," he says with a bit of twang that I fully expected from a man in this part of the country, especially in this setting.

I walk over to him. I pull a folded piece of paper from my pocket and unfurl it on the counter. "Well, I just moved into a place a couple miles from here, over on 1250 East, and I need a few things to get the cabin cleaned up and ready to live in."

He pulls the list toward him and quickly reads through it. "We got most of this ... Miss?"

"Annie. You can call me Annie. And who might you be?"

"David Farmer, but my friends just call me Farmer. I own the place, so says the sign on the building."

"And the sons?"

"You looking for a date, Miss Annie?"

I chuckle. "Oh gosh no. I was just curious."

"Well, as it turns out, I jumped the gun on naming this place as there were no sons to be had, and my two daughters left this red neck town a long time ago."

"I see."

"Not a lot of people actually move into this town. Mostly out. I take it you're not from around here?"

"Pennsylvania, primarily."

"Never been. Anyhow, welcome to Burton, the most boring place in the world."

"Boring is fine by me. I could use a little normal."

"We got that in spades darling. As for this list, we have most of this too. A few things you'll have to get at the IGA."

"That's great. Oh crap. Before I forget, I was told that someone here could service the propane generator and the solar panels at the cabin. Do you know who that is?"

"Bernard does that. He works for me. Let me guess, you up at the 10500 place ... on 1250 east, right?"

"Yep."

"Tom's old place. I know it well. Did you know Tom? Haven't seen him in a few years."

"Tom was a good friend of mine. He passed away recently. Heart failure. He gave me the cabin."

"Oh dear. I'm sorry to hear that. We played poker when he was around. Great guy. He'll be missed, for sure."

"Yeah, he meant a lot to me. His cabin is giving me a chance to start over, which is nice, but it's bittersweet."

"Welp, let me call Bernard and I'll get him over there right away. As for this list, let me make a copy and gather up all this stuff while you pop over to the grocery store to get the rest. It'll take me thirty minutes or so. Will that do?"

"That would be great. Thank you so much."

Farmer turns around and uses a small all-in-printer to make a copy of my list. He then grabs a nearby pen and circles a few items on the original list. "These here are the ones we don't have."

"Again, thank you. I'll just, uh, head over there and get that other stuff, then I'll be back shortly. Much appreciated."

"Pleasure. Is there a good time for Bernard to stop over today?"

"I'd say any time after one would be fine."

"Okay, I'll let him know. You have a phone number I can give him? That way he can call when he's on his way over."

"Of course. Let me see that copy of the list." He slides it over with the pen. I write down my name and cell phone number at the top. "I will see you when I'm done."

He gives me a quick wave and picks up the list.

I head out the door. I can see the IGA on the corner, across the street and to my left, so I decide to just walk over instead of taking the car.

The store is small but efficient, brightly lit, and super clean. It appears to have everything a bigger one might carry, only a lot less brands and not nearly as much inventory. I noticed when I entered there were only three checkout lanes, one cashier, and a manager behind the service area.

I find a few decent looking gala apples, a bag of Idaho potatoes, and some prewashed and cut lettuce. By the time I get to the hardware and household aisle, I've also managed to pick up some deli meat, mustard, pumpernickel bread, a dozen eggs, some milk, several pounds of bacon and three steaks, and a few boxes of k-cups.

The items I need from my big list that Farmer didn't have will be in this aisle. I quickly find the single cup coffee brewer, a pack of dish towels, a box of zipper bags, a bottle of dish soap, and my favorite toilet paper.

I can't remember the last time I shopped like this. At the Kill House, we had everything delivered and never had to worry about the basic necessities. Me standing here behind a big shopping cart, filling it with TP and dish soap is just so ... domestic. It feels right, though. Weird, yes, but right.

At the checkout, the cashier greets me with a big smile and a hello. Her name tag says Becky. I place all the items on the conveyor belt. She scans the items and they accumulate at the end.

"Looks like a new apartment starter kit you got going here," Becky says.

"Close. Just moved into a cabin a few miles from here. Can't live without the coffee, that's for sure."

"Sweet tea person myself. No matter how many times I've tried, I could never get past the bitterness of coffee. No amount of sugar does the trick."

"Fair enough. I'm Annie, by the way. I imagine we'll be seeing each other from time to time."

"Nice to meet you. I'm Becky. I work days Tuesday through Saturday." She scans the deli meat. "My husband Jake runs the diner down the street, if you ever need an awesome piece of pie. I mean, they got other good food too, but the baker, Phyliss makes the best damn pie in this county."

"Thank you. I'll definitely give it a shot. I need two small bags of ice too."

She scans the final item, enters a code for the ice, and hits

ENTER on the register. "Your total comes to two fifty-four and eighty-two cents."

I pull a wad of money from the cargo pocket on my right leg. I separate thirteen, twenty-dollar bills from my stash and hand them over.

She puts the bills into the drawer, grabs my change, and counts it out to me. She quickly moves down to bag up the groceries.

I walk around to the end and take the coffee machine, placing it into the cart. I also help out by taking the bags as she finishes each one.

"You have a great day, Annie. Come back and see us."

"I will. Thank you."

I get the two bags of ice from the freezer near the exit and put them on the bottom of the cart. I have too many bags and other stuff to carry, so I decide to keep the cart. Once I load the backseat of my car, I return the cart, then jog back over to Farmer's. It dawns on me that I should probably ditch the car I have and find something new. Old habits die hard, but in this case, it may be necessary, at least once more.

Inside the hardware store, I find Farmer behind the counter and a flatbed cart nearby, presumably with all my goods stacked three feet high.

"Holy crap! Did I buy all that?"

"Not yet you haven't."

I look at him and he smiles. I glance back at the cart and see all the things I wanted, including a broom, mop, paper towels, vacuum, various cleaning fluids, charcoal briquets, and another two dozen items.

"What's the damage?"

"Well, considering how much you bought ... and that I hope to see you in here frequently, I rounded down to four hundred even."

"How nice. Thanks. But you didn't have to do that."

"We look out for our own. You never know, one day I may need a favor from you. Hopefully you'll remember good ol' Farmer."

"Ohhhh, I see what you're doing. Hoping I bake cookies or make a mean lasagna or something, right? Is that what you're up to?"

"Not specifically, but I sure won't object to either option." He gives me a big wink. "And, on account of you making such a large first purchase, I wasn't sure what you had up at the cabin for basic tools, so I went ahead and threw together a few things inside that little red toolbox there on the bottom. Tape measure, hammer, some wrenches and screwdrivers. Never know what you might need."

"You're too kind, Mr. Farmer. Thanks again." I turn slightly and get the money ready. I turn back and place the cash on the counter. "Any luck with Bernard?"

"He'll be there around 2 today. He'll call when he's on his way."

"Great. I'll be knee deep in cleaning mode for the next couple of days, and it'll be nice to get that generator situation taken care of, in case it turns cold."

"There's probably a wood pile around the back of the cabin, but in case it's all wet, grab a few of those bundles sitting out front when you leave. Something to get you started anyway."

"I think I could get used to this. It's been awhile since someone has been so nice to me."

I'm already forming a fake backstory to tell these people that involves leaving an abusive situation, hence all the cash and need for privacy. Hopefully, they'll buy it when the time comes.

"Like I said, we take care of our own. Call if you ever need anything. Make sure you open the flue before using the fireplace or you'll smoke yourself out of there and cause a fire."

"Good tip." I give him a thumbs up. "I'll go load this stuff up and bring back the cart."

"Nonsense. I'll help you load up."

I don't bother to try and talk him out of it. He won't take

no for an answer anyway.

I put the refrigerated food in the Coleman cooler I bought from Farmer and then dump the ice in. We fill up the trunk and the backseat of my car with the rest of the stuff and I use the opportunity to ask another favor.

"I need to get rid of this car and get something different. If you know of anyone selling a good, used vehicle, preferably something small, under five-grand, let me know, will ya?"

"I'll put some feelers out there. Something wrong with this one?"

"Not really. Just looking for a little anonymity. Don't want anyone from my past sneaking up on me."

He gives me a queer eye. "Anything or anyone in particular I should be looking out for?"

"I doubt it. He has no idea where I am. Just being cautious."

"Okay then. Be careful out there. Those boxes of ammo you bought make a lot more sense now."

I shrug and shut the car door. "I better get started with all that cleaning." I walk around to the driver's side.

He nods and starts pushing the cart back to the front door.

I get in and drive away, fully content with my morning errands. I leave with a deep sense of satisfaction, ready and eager to bleach the shit out of that cabin and start to make it a home.

19

I'm anxious to get the cabin cleaned up, but as I drive down these country roads on my way there from the hardware store, I find myself going a little under the speed limit just to take in the scenery. For the first time in as long as I can remember, I'm in no rush to get somewhere. I can simply drive, enjoy the view, and breathe clearly and calmly.

I've already made a few friends in town and I'm feeling safer by the minute. I won't get complacent though. Can't afford to do that. I still have my trusty firearms which I will strategically place around the property in case the day ever comes I need to face down an AWT assassin. I hope it never comes to that. I know they will never stop looking for me, not so long as Madame K is in power, but this world is a big ol' place. Good luck assholes. If I can stay alive long enough to get past her reign, I just might have a chance.

I turn down the final road to my cabin. I glance over to my left and spot something moving near a small grove of trees. My mind immediately goes the wrong way, but whatever it is, it's not human. I pull off to the side of the road, just to be cautious.

My eyes are fixed on the overgrowth. There are a shit-ton of deer out here, and I'm sure raccoons, possum, foxes, and the like. I pull a gun from the glove box, check it for ammo, then get out of the car, leaving it running. I stuff the piece into the front waist of my pants and cross the street, checking both directions for traffic, of which there is absolutely none.

I see movement again. From behind a tree emerges a scraggily looking dog that is in desperate need of a bath. Luckily for him or her, the dominate breed of this mutt is short-haired. If I had to guess, I'd say it's a pointer mixed with something smaller, like a beagle, as it's a little smaller than the average English Pointer. I'm no expert but I've been to enough shelters to have seen some strange combos. His head is mostly brown, his body and legs are a combination of brown and white with small brown spots in random places.

The dog just stands there staring at me, not aggressive in any way, but cautious. I squat down to seem less intimidating and offer my hand. I'm probably twenty feet away. He's curious but doesn't budge. I move a few feet closer. He stays put.

"Hello little guy. Are you lost?" I use my best baby talk voice. Upon hearing me speak, the dog takes a few steps back. I can see the dog has no collar or tags. Could be abandoned or lost.

It dawns on me I have some deli meat in the car, so I slowly stand, inching backwards. "You must be hungry. I'll be right back. Please don't run away."

I turn and cross the street, get into the back seat of the car and dig out the package of ham, and return to the spot I was standing originally on the other side. I crouch down and unzip the bag, pulling out a single thin slice of the black forest ham. I dangle it out in front of me.

"You want some ham?"

The dog waves his nose in the air and gets a whiff, instantly piquing his interest.

"I'm not going to bring it to you. You need to come closer to me if you want this." I toss the piece of ham and it lands five feet in front of the dog.

Without hesitation, the dog practically leaps on the ham

and gobbles it up. He looks right to me after, wanting more.

I get another slice and toss it to a place ten feet from me. I do this twice more, halving the distance each time, and each time the dog eats the ham. I can see now he is a boy dog and he's within petting distance if I were to reach forward. His eyes are fixated on the bag of ham, and rightfully so.

With my left hand, I hide the bag behind me, and I extend my right hand, knuckles up, to let him sniff me and test his friendliness.

He cranes his head forward, sniffs my hand, smelling mostly ham, then proceeds to lick the fingers until they are soaked with dog slobber. All the while, his tail is wagging mid-height with a broad width, which should mean he is accepting of me.

"That's such a good boy. You must have been starving."

I take a chance and move my hand to his chin and give it a brief rub. He accepts but still tries to lick my fingers. I move to his cheek area and scratch, eventually moving to the top of his head, where he allows me to pet him front to back three times. I retreat.

"I don't know why you're out here all alone, and other than being dirty and hungry, you look fine." I stand up. He sits and looks up at me, wanting more ham. I give him two more slices. "I want you to come home with me. Okay? You're going to need a bath but you can stay with me until we figure out where you belong, if you belong anywhere. Okay? Come on."

I cross the street and he follows right along like we've always known each other and are long lost pals. I can't help but smile with delight. I realize I'll have to go back to town tomorrow to pick up some proper dog food and a doggie bed, but for tonight I can make him eggs and I suppose I can give up some of my steak. Lucky little shit.

I jog around to the passenger side and open the door. He stands nearby looking at me.

"You want more ham, you gotta get in." I shake the bag then tap the seat of the car. "Go on. Get in."

He seems to understand and jumps right in.

"Good boy!" I shut the door and rush around to the other side. Once inside, I give him another piece of ham, return the gun to the glove box, and drive away.

He's been sitting patiently as we arrive at the cabin. In the few minutes of drivetime, I kept glancing over to him to see if I could figure out what a good name would be for him. If I had to guess, he's not very old, and other than being dirty, he's not scrapped up or injured in any obvious way. That leads me to believe he hasn't been on his own long. I found him on the side of the road. Hmmm. Roadie. That's not bad. Roadie.

"Hey, Roadie." He turns to me, tongue wagging. "Okay then. You will now be Roadie. That was easy."

Twenty minutes pass as I unload the car. Roadie found the couch and immediately plopped down and made himself comfortable. I guess that's his spot now. That's okay. He can have it. He's probably been sleeping in the dirt for weeks. I'll give him a bath later to fix that problem, but for now, I have work to do to make this place livable.

I place a small Bluetooth speaker that I brought on the kitchen counter. Using a radio app on my phone, I choose a 90s playlist and set it loose on the cabin.

I look around and try to figure out the best way to tackle this big job. I decide the best approach, at least to start, is to clean the bathroom top-to-bottom. That will give me a tremendous sense of accomplishment and somewhere I can feel comfortable taking a bath. I'll then wash the dog so he's not running around spreading the filth.

After that, I'll wipe every surface down in the bedroom, living room, and kitchen area, and that includes the inside of all the appliances and washing all the dishes. By then I'll be ready for some lunch and a break, so I'll do that while I wait for the generator guy to get here.

Once he leaves, I'll be able to vacuum the furniture and the floors, check the lightbulbs, and once the refrigerator is down to temperature, transfer the food from the cooler.

I figure by that point, I'll be exhausted and ready to quit for the day, so I'll leave the outdoor stuff for tomorrow. That involves cleaning the grill and washing down the patio furniture, clearing the cobwebs, leaves, and branches from the front and back porches, and assessing if there are any repairs that might be needed on the exterior.

I'll go into town again and get Roadie's supplies, maybe have a meal at the diner, and grab more ham, considering the new pooch ate half my supply.

It's going to be a busy couple of days, but after all that mess is done, I'll be able to relax and just enjoy this place.

20

For some reason, I awake suddenly. The room is dark. I use the backlight on my watch and find it to be 2:38 in the morning. Then I hear the tiniest rumble, like an engine idling but almost too far away to make out. I hear it again, then realize what it is. Roadie is in the living room and growling at something. Maybe he found a mouse under the couch.

I get out of bed, grabbing my cell phone to use as a flashlight. Halfway to the bedroom door, the floorboards on the front porch creak, the leaves and branches on it rustling around like feet shuffling through.

I put the phone in my pocket and grab the rifle I have leaning up against the dresser to my right. I left it loaded so I don't bother checking. With the barrel out in front of me, I make it to the doorframe and stop. I can see Roadie standing about four feet from the front door, rigid, tail as high and firm as it can get. He's releasing small, low two-second growls. The movement on the porch continues.

I whisper, "Roadie, come here." At first, he doesn't respond, so I go deeper and more authoritative with my voice and repeat my command. "Roadie, come ... here ... now." He obeys and comes to my side, still on red alert.

My first thoughts about what might be happening are

related to AWT. Did they find me? Doesn't seem likely. I suppose it's possible they found out about Tom and the property and his recent death. No one at the company has ever mentioned Tom to me, so I don't think they know, but I could be wrong. Prior to my recruitment, I have no idea how long they'd been watching, or at least how long Madame K had been.

I take a deep breath and choose to bury the idea. I decided recently I would try to manifest my reality by thinking only of the best-case scenarios. I don't know how much I believe in that kind of mind-over-matter stuff. For now, I'm going to live it.

I debate whether I should yell something to try and scare off the intruder or just surprise them. If it's an AWT person, the yelling won't matter. I'll be dead before the words leave my mouth.

I creep toward the entrance, and with the rifle resting in my left hand, I unlock the door and twist the knob as quietly as I can, then pull it open swiftly, releasing the knob to enable a full grip on the rifle.

I jump back a step. To my surprise, a full-grown doe is on the left side of the porch, facing the street. She turns her head for the briefest of moments before bolting away into the darkness.

Roadie runs past me and out into the front yard, barking a few times. He stops running just before getting to the street. He barks a few more times, gives out a little howl, then turns back to me.

My heart rate had escalated without my noticing. I let out a huge sigh of relief as I lower the weapon. I step out to the porch and look around in all directions. I don't see or hear anything unusual. Fuckin' wildlife. This is the kind of nonsense that makes people piss their pants.

"Come here, boy. Just a deer. Just a fucking deer. Let's go back to bed."

Roadie lets out a few more barks, then trots over to me. I pet him on the top of his head. "Good boy. You make a great alarm system. Ain't nobody gonna be sneakin' up on us."

We enter the cabin and I take one last look outside, then I shut and lock the door. I rub my eyes and yawn. I'm still tired but need the adrenaline to fade or getting into bed won't do much good.

I return the rifle to where I found it and use the bathroom. After I finish peeing, I wash my hands. When I see my reflection in the mirror, there's something odd. I notice the blonde of my hair is fading fast. I hadn't paid much attention the last few weeks. That's not the weird thing though, just noticeable. With some of my memories now intact and the fact I now have a photograph of her, I don't see Josey Baldwin anymore. What I see is Annie Jones, or at least some crossbred of her and Kiki. It's almost as if my personal identity is morphing, not physically so much, but in my head. This realization can only help me going forward. Finding a new person to be while trying to escape the past is okay by me. Of course, I'm not really finding a new person. It's more like I'm discovering who I really am, or maybe I'm finally experiencing who I would have become if circumstances had been different.

I return to bed and find Roadie curled up on the end. I crawl back under the covers, roll over to my left side, and my eyes get heavy in a matter of minutes.

21

The chill in the air this morning left me wanting to just stay in bed all day, curled up under the comforter with a full pot of coffee and a book. Unfortunately, I need to run into to town and get Roadie his supplies before he ends up eating all my food. Plus, after all that physical activity from yesterday's cleaning marathon, I woke up starving, and I can't think of a better thing to do right now than treat myself to big ass omelet with at least two sides of crispy bacon.

So here I am driving at eight a.m. to the diner. I left Roadie at home to guard the property. I won't feel right taking him anywhere until I get him a collar and a leash. I'll also ask around town to see if anyone knows Roadie or where he might have come from. I don't want to steal someone else's dog. If I can, I'll even print up some flyers to pin up around town saying that I found a lost dog. If no one comes forward within thirty days, he'll stay with me. After that, I'll take him to a vet.

The streets are quiet as I drive. I pass a school bus and maybe two other cars on the way to town. I reach the diner, aptly named, A Small Diner, as it looks like it might seat forty people, ten of which would be at the long counter separating the kitchen from the rest of the seating. I park and enter the restaurant, surprised to find a dozen patrons. Being the only place like this in town, I guess I shouldn't be surprised that most of the people who live around here would be frequent patrons.

"Sit wherever you like, honey," a woman about my height says. She's probably in her sixties with a full head of gray hair that is rolled into a bun on the top of her head. "I'll be there in just a sec." She hustles away to fill coffees and hand out checks.

I glance at all the seating and see three empty spots at the end of the counter on the far end. I walk over and take the second to last one. I pull a menu from the middle of the napkin and salt and pepper shaker holder and give it a quick read. They have the usual dirty spoon items. Before I realize it, the waitress is front of me.

"I'm Tammy. I'll be takin' care of you today. Can I start you off with somethin' to drink?"

"Hi, Tammy. I'd love some coffee with half and half, if you got it."

"We sure do. I don't remember seeing you in here before. Passing through or sticking around?"

"Hopefully sticking around. I'm Annie. You remember a Tom Ichiro? Had a cabin a little ways from here."

"Sure, sure. Ol' Tom. You know him?"

"Yeah. He was a good friend of mine. He passed recently and left me his cabin. I'll be staying there for a while."

"Oh," she says, her face turning sour. "I'm sorry to hear that, hun. He was a nice fella. Big tipper. Every time he stayed at the cabin, he would bring me a little jade animal figurine. I have like ten of them now."

Those jade figurines belonged to Tom's wife before she passed. There were dozens of them around the house. His wife was half Chinese, half Japanese, so she would find four or five of them every time they visited China. Tom must have been really fond of Tammy to have given her those. Little flirt.

"He must have liked you a lot to give those up." I decide

not to mention they belonged to his wife. I doubt he told her. "He would never give one to *me*." I smile wide and give her a wink.

"Well, I'll sure miss him around here."

I can see her face evolve into a deeper sadness as she fights to hold onto her normally cheery demeanor. There may have been something more between them, perhaps never fully expressed. Potential love unknown and unpursued. How depressing.

"The world was definitely better with him in it." I need to break the awkward tension. "I can, ummm ... order now if you're ready."

She nods. "Absolutely." She readies her pen.

"I'd love a three-egg omelet with ham and swiss, two sides of bacon, crispy, no bread or potatoes."

"Gotcha. Anything else?"

"Nope. Thank you."

"I'll get this in and get your coffee." She walks away.

I turn slightly so I can see the comings and goings of the diner. There's light chatter, sipping, silverware clanking on plates, and all the sounds of a kitchen at breakfast time. For the first time in a long time, I realize I'm simply enjoying my surroundings and not paranoid that some crazed assassin or Battle Boy might blow through the door and attack me. I'm almost a little verklempt over it. Almost, but not quite.

The minutes pass as I guzzle coffee, eat my omelet, and slowly savor each and every bite of the best bacon I can remember eating.

When Tammy returns with the check, I decide to inquire about their world-famous pie.

"I was told by Becky over at the IGA that the pie in this place is the best there is. I'd love to take a piece home for later. What's available?"

"We have coconut crème, chocolate silk, apple, and pumpkin all the time. This month's specials are cherry and peach."

"Choices, choices. I could eat all of them. How about we

do pumpkin and cherry, one piece of each to try. Thanks."

"Great. I'll add those to the ticket and be right back with 'em."

I smile and nod.

A few minutes later, Tammy returns with two Styrofoam containers and my check.

"You come back and see us."

"I will. Give my compliments to the chef on his perfectly prepared bacon."

"Just pay at the register, hun. Jake'll take care of ya."

"Okay. Thanks for the pie."

Tammy bolts off with her coffee pot in hand, ready to dish out the refills.

I look at the check. Nineteen dollar and twelve cents? Wow. And that's with two pieces of pie. I haven't paid so little for a meal at a sit-down restaurant, probably ever. This is going to become a thing with me now, I can just tell.

I pull some folded bills from my right pants pocket, find a twenty and a five, leaving the five pinned under my coffee mug.

I rise and head to the cash register. There's no line so I step right up. A man I presume is Jake puts up an index finger to me. He's on the phone nearby. Once he hangs up, he comes right over.

"Everything okay with your meal?"

"Wonderful, yes. I can't wait to try this pie later."

"Phyliss has a way with crust. You won't be disappointed. Tammy says you're new around here, living up at Tom's old place. Sad he won't be around anymore. He ate here every day when he visited."

"I am, and yes, Tom left a hole in our lives, that's for sure. Are you Jake? I'm Annie, by the way."

"I am. I run this place."

"I know. I met your wife yesterday at the IGA. She sent me your way."

"Good. Nice to have a new face around here. You ever need anything, just let us know. We live just two blocks down

Main Street, left on Cobalt, third house on the left."

"Thanks. I appreciate that. Everyone's been super nice in Burton."

Jake rings up my bill and states the total. I give over the twenty and he returns my eighty-eight cents.

"You have a nice day and come back and see us soon."

"Thank, Jake. I will. Oh, I almost forgot. Do you know of anyone missing a dog? I found a lost one not far from my cabin. Kind of a pointer-beagle mix, mostly brown and white with little brown spots. No collar. Looks like he'd been on his own for at least a few weeks."

"Hmmm. I haven't heard anything. Lot of people have dogs around here and I'm sure I would have heard something if one were missing. Then again, a lot of people from the bigger cities around here will drop off the animals they don't want in the middle of the countryside. That's probably what you're looking at."

"Yeah, never thought of that. If you happen to hear anything, let me know. I'm going to keep him unless someone comes along and claims him. He's a sweet dog."

"I'll do that. Have a good one." Jake walks away, I'm sure with a list of a hundred things to do in a busy diner.

I give a quick wave and leave the restaurant. I decide to hit the hardware store and the IGA to further inquire about any missing dogs and see if Farmer can help me get a few flyers printed up to hang around town. I know he has a computer and a printer, and I'm sure he won't mind giving me a little assist.

I park right in front of Farmer's and go into the building, the pieces of pie in my hand. Never hurts to have a dessert to use as a convincer when asking someone for a favor.

There's no one behind the counter but I guarantee that bell above the door made Farmer aware a customer had arrived.

"I'll be right there in just a minute to help you out," Farmer yells from an unknown location near the back of the store.

I yell back, "Take your time. It's just me, Annie."

I walk over and lean against the counter, surveying all the shelves of the store. For a small-town place, his inventory is impressive. Of course, there are enough rural towns around here with people that would just as soon come here than have to go to a big box store in the city.

A minute later, Farmer emerges from the back.

"Didn't expect to see you back in here so soon. Everything okay? Bernard get you squared away?"

"Oh yeah, thank you. Generator working perfectly. That combined with the solar panels on the back of the roof, I should have an abundance of electricity." I place the Styrofoam containers on the counter.

"Well, good."

"What I'm really here for is your computer."

"Oh?"

"I found a dog on the side of the road near the cabin. Medium sized pointer-beagle mix. No collar or tags or anything."

"Hmmm. Happens a lot out here. People can't handle their animals, they drop 'em off in the country. So, what you need the computer for?"

"I'm going to keep him. I call him Roadie. But before I take official possession of him, I'd like to at least print a few flyers and post them around to make sure someone isn't just missing their dog. Think you could help me out with that? I'd be happy to pay for your time and the printing cost."

"Oh sure. I print ads all the time to put up on the windows or bulletin boards of the other businesses. We can just use one of them and modify it. Come around the counter here and I'll get the computer up."

I follow him to the other side. He offers me a bar stool. He takes the desk chair and boots up the laptop.

"You got a picture of Roadie?"

"It's on my phone." I thought ahead and brought the USB cord with me. I pull the cord from my pocket, handing it and the phone to him.

Once the laptop is fully loaded, he plugs them both in and rises from his chair. "Switch me seats. You can probably do this faster and easier than I can."

We swap chairs and as I work on copying the picture and making the flyer, I figure this might be a good time to ask another favor, although, I realize I may be pushing my luck.

"So, you wouldn't happen to need a little help around the store, would ya? I could really use a part-time job."

"Know your way around a dual-bevel sliding compound miter saw and a sprinkler system solenoid valve?"

"I don't even know what you just said, but I can run the register, do computer stuff, sweep, and just generally hang around and be cute." I give him my best cheesy fake wide smile. I can also fuck people up who try and steal shit or break in. I'll just keep that little tidbit out of this impromptu interview.

"Not that there isn't value in ... being cute, I just don't know how much that's worth around here. Sweeping maybe. My back hurts like a sumbitch most days."

"I should mention, before you get too attached, I would need this to be an under-the-table type deal." I rub my lips and grimace. "I'm coming from a complicated situation and I can't have anyone finding out where I'm at or I will literally end up dead. No joke."

"Well, Miss Annie, that comes with risks for me too, ya know."

"I know." I give a quick couple of nods. "I fully understand if you won't do it, but it would be a huge favor to me. You wouldn't have to pay me much. It's not really about the money anyway. I just need something normal to do, help me feel like a part of the real world again."

Farmer sighs and looks me straight in the eyes. I can tell he's trying to search for the soul behind my eyes. I think there's one in there but who knows. I just hope he doesn't look too deep. He'd shit himself if he could see the things I've done.

"Alright, Miss Annie. Here's the deal. What I really need is help toward the evening. We're open from seven to five, Tuesday through Saturday. The last few hours of the day on Tuesday, Wednesday, and Thursday is when it really slows down. If I could leave at three on those days and have you here to cover, that might work. I'm always a phone call away if people have questions you can't answer."

"That sounds perfect, Mr. Farmer. Thank you so much."

"And we're going to consider this a seasonal situation. We'll reevaluate after the holidays are over. And I might need you here on a few Saturdays during November and December."

"No problem at all. Happy to help out." I'm just about finished typing up the flyer and ready to print.

"Good. I can give you seven-fifty an hour. That's it. That's coming right out of my own pocket."

"I understand. That's very generous." I select twenty copies to print and the printer comes to life with a lot of buzzing and whirring. Finally, pages begin to emerge. I disconnect the phone from the laptop and return it and the USB cord to my pocket.

Farmer grabs the printouts from the tray and examines the top one. "Looks like you're all set. Oh wait." He hands me the flyers and turns to the counter, finding a shallow box on the shelf beneath the register. He takes something from it and returns the box. He turns and hands the yellow and black staple gun to me. "You'll need this. Just bring it back when you're done with it."

"Oh yeah. Thanks. Much appreciated. You might just be the nicest person I've ever met, Farmer. I owe you a debt."

"Like I'm sure I've mentioned, we take care of each other 'round here. You'll find a way to pay it forward."

"I could get used to this place. The people are undeniably great, and you're kinda growing on me too." I give him a wink.

"Like moss creeping up on the shady side of the house. Once it's there, it's a bitch to get rid of." He smiles.

I point at him. "You said that, not me." I smile back. I

come around to the customer side of the counter. "You like pumpkin or cherry pie better."

"Always been a pumpkin guy myself. Why?"

I slide the container containing the piece of pumpkin pie across the counter to him. "Then that's for you. Thanks for your help." I grab my piece and turn to leave.

I can hear him open the container. I glance back and see him pick up the slice and take a huge bite of it. He chews fast and swallows.

"Phyllis makes the best," he says.

I raise my left fist in solidarity and leave the store, grateful to have a job and a friend. As I get to my car, I realize I'm actually a little reluctant to put up the flyers. I want to keep Roadie. Hopefully no one calls. I'll do the right thing, of course, but I don't have to like it.

22

Six weeks later...

A few weeks ago, I spent a week decorating the hardware store for Halloween. Farmer informed me that he doesn't usually do much aside from putting a plastic jack o' lantern full of mini candy bars on the counter for the customers to enjoy. I convinced him to allow me to hang a plastic skeleton in the front window along with some resin pumpkins, some fake cobwebs, and a large black cauldron full of pumpkin carving kits to make people aware we have them for sale. I threw a couple of other things around the store to complete the ensemble, including several strands of orange LED lights.

I don't think Farmer had any interest but he tends to indulge me if I give him the puppy dog eyes and a pouty bottom lip. I don't abuse it but it's nice to know I have the technique in my back pocket.

Another great benefit of working at the hardware store is having Roadie here with me. I brought Roadie in to meet Farmer and they became fast friends, and after a few days trial run of seeing how Roadie would interact with random customers coming and going from the store, he passed the test for workplace companion. Plus, Farmer liked the idea of

Roadie being here with me when I'm working alone. It's so adorable when Farmer is being protective of me. If he only knew. I can't help but chuckle at the shit he doesn't know about me. Hopefully, he'll never find out. His heart would break into a million pieces.

I'm here on a Thursday night, Halloween night, and business is slow. Roadie is asleep in the bed I put behind the counter for him. He's snoring, obnoxiously so. I'm glad he can rest through the boredom. I, on the other hand, am crawling out of my skin for something new to do.

Despite the fact that trick or treating doesn't officially start until five p.m., the exact time we close, I've been told some folks will bring their kids around to get candy from the local downtown businesses between four-thirty and five. It's twenty minutes until five and still no kiddies. I keep walking over to the door to look for tiny versions of the latest costume sensations. Finally, I spot a small group of kids with two adults right behind emerging from the IGA.

After hitting a few other businesses, the group finally arrives here. The doorbell does nothing to wake Roadie but the giggling does the trick. He springs from his bed, tail wagging furiously as he runs from around the counter to great our guests.

I grab the candy bucket and follow him to the door. I greet the adults with a smile, then turn my attention to the littles. If I had to guess, they're between seven and eleven years old.

And they're beyond adorable. We have a Wonder Woman, a unicorn fairy, best as I can tell, and a light-saber wielding character from one of the Star Wars movies. I haven't seen the last few, so I have no idea which one.

"You guys are just the cutest."

"What do you say?" the female chaperone asks of the children.

A chorus of cute 'trick o' treats' fill my ears. Afraid that no one else will show up, I grab huge handfuls of candy and place them in each one of their bags. The boy has the typical plastic jack o' lantern, while the girls are sporting custom made cloth sacks that perfectly match their outfits.

The little girl in the unicorn fairy outfit's eyes go wide when she realizes how much candy I gave her.

"Thank you," she says.

"You're very welcome and I love your fairy wings."

She smiles, coyly. She swings her hips to show them off. "They're trans-blue-cent," she stammers out.

I'm sure she's meant translucent, but they do in fact have a blue sheen, so maybe she said exactly what she intended to.

"They sure are. Have a safe evening and don't eat too much candy."

The chaperones thank me and usher the kids back out of the door, on to their next destination.

I go back to the counter. I return the bucket to its place. Roadie is right beside me. I give him a scratch on the head. I casually straighten up some of the crap sitting on the counter. For some reason, I get a chill up my spine. What's the saying about that? When you feel that, it's someone walking over your future gravesite? Appropriate, I suppose, considering the holiday. But no, that's not it. What I'm sensing is eyes on me. I have a peculiar knack for it, which is no shock with my upbringing.

I turn around and about jump out of my skin. Someone is sporting the white ghost face and black robe costume from the Scream movies. I settle down quickly and brush my hand across my face, a sort of emotional reset. When Roadie sees him, he gets into instant defense mode, drops his head, and starts releasing slow growls. I give the jokester a smirk to say I'm not impressed.

He doesn't move an inch, a valiant attempt to unnerve me, but he has no idea who he's dealing with. I've done things to people that if he witnessed them, he'd quite literally shit his pants. Oh, these little boys who pretend to be men.

I shoo him away with my left hand.

He remains still.

Roadie's growling intensifies.

"It's okay, boy. He's just being a creep."

The guy cocks his head to the side, slowly.

I almost laugh. I'll give him credit though, he's bought in.

I shout, "That costume is like ten years too late, hillbilly."

He raises his left arm and reveals a large, all-black hunting knife. Believe me, I know my knives, and that thing is no Halloween prop, it's the real deal. And now he's just pissing me off.

I pick up the store phone and mimic dialing 9-1-1 as I mouth the numbers. Instead of bailing, he steps up our little game and takes the tip of the knife and drags it across the glass at neck level to simulate slicing someone's throat. The screeching noise makes my eardrums want to explode and forces a weird bark from Roadie.

Fun time is officially over. Now I'm going to have to fuck this little asshole up.

I turn around and return the phone to its base. When I face the door again, he's gone.

"That's what I thought you little bitch," I shout.

I rush over to the door to make sure it's not damaged. There's the tiniest of lines about twelve inches wide. Farmer is going to be pissed.

I pull the door open and hit the sidewalk, looking in all directions for the robed vandal. He's nowhere to be found. I think briefly about running up and down the street to find him, if for no other reason than to bust his ass for scratching the door, but I can't leave the store unattended, so I stay put.

Should I call the cops? I doubt I've ever asked that question before. With my fake identity, I don't know if I can even do that. I hate to call Farmer with such a minor thing, but he might be angry if I don't. Fuck.

Back in the store, I notice it's now ten minutes after five, so I lock the door, finish my duties, then pick up the phone and dial Farmer.

"Hey, Farm, it's Annie."

"Everything okay? Give out any candy?"

"A few kids popped in but that's it. I'm calling because

some asshole played a little prank and it resulted in the front door of the store getting a small scratch across the glass." My tone almost suggests I'm making an excuse for the offender. I don't mean to. I must be making an effort to soften the blow to Farmer in hopes it doesn't get blown out of proportion.

"There's always at least one group of high schoolers that egg the shop, or TP the entire downtown, or something. How bad is it? Will the door need replaced?"

"Not bad. Barely a surface scratch. The door will be fine. If you didn't know it was there already, you might not even notice it." He's being more chill about this than I expected.

"You see who it was?"

"No. They had on a Halloween mask, of course. Ran away when I started to get pissed off."

"Don't worry about it then. You 'bout ready to pack up and head home?"

"I am. Last thing was to call you."

"If you don't have any plans, why don't you stop by for dinner. I'm not much of a cook ... in fact, I mostly eat at the diner, but I made a big batch of chili with no one to share it with. Kind of a tradition in this house from when Evelyn was alive and the girls were still at home."

I don't really want to go over, but Jesus, after that last bit, how can I refuse.

"I'd love to. Thanks. I haven't had chili in years. Can I stop by the IGA and grab something?"

"Not unless you need something to drink other than coffee, sweet tea, or water."

"How about a Phyliss pie?"

"If it's not too much trouble."

"It's on the way. Pumpkin seems appropriate. You okay with that?"

"My fav. I'll see you soon then?"

"Shouldn't be more than thirty minutes, depending on how busy the diner is."

"Good. Bye."

"Bye." I hang up the phone, grab my bag, and go through

my usual exit routine.

I drive over to the IGA first, leaving Roadie in the car. I need to pick him up a can of dog food and grab a diet soda. I'll grab the pie after this and head over to Farmer's house. I know where he lives but I've yet to actually visit. It's a gorgeous, white, turn-of-the-century house with a green metal roof, about three miles from the store. It still has a giant carriage house that has since been converted to a four-car garage. I look forward to checking out the interior. Hopefully, the character matches the outside. I tend to favor more modern homes, but for some reason, I'm a sucker for a big ol' farmhouse. My mood instantly improves at the prospect, something to turn this evening's bullshit into a positive memory.

23

With pie and a plastic grocery bag in hand and Roadie at my side, I ring the doorbell at Farmer's house. The door is a wood stained shade of cherry with a beautifully ornate glass insert in the top third, like waves of the ocean moving sideways.

The porch is exactly what I thought it would be, extending for twenty feet to either side, enclosed with a short white rail. To my right, there is a teak swing hanging from the ceiling. The other side has four teak rocking chairs, all unfinished and weathered.

The door opens and Farmer greets me with a smile. "Come on in."

I walk through the threshold, Roadie in tow, and Farmer shuts the door behind us. I'm instantly in awe of all the original woodwork and hardwood floors. "Your home is gorgeous. Wow."

"Thank you. It's been updated quite a bit but we left as much of the original trim and stuff as we could. It wouldn't have the same character without it. The kitchen is a different story. We completely modernized it. They designed kitchens so much differently a hundred years ago. Let me take that from you."

I hand over the pie. He walks us out of the foyer, down a short hallway to the back of the house where the kitchen is.

He wasn't kidding about modern. The cabinets are all white shaker, the pulls are chrome, the counters a grayish marble, the appliances stainless, and the floor is a smoky gray porcelain tile that looks a lot like hardwood. Stunning.

From nowhere, the chili powder, cumin, and tomatoes hit my nose. "Good gravy that smells delicious." Roadie doesn't leave my side. In an unfamiliar place, he is over-protective.

"Tried and true recipe." Farmer places the pie on the counter between the stove and the fridge. "Any of that need to be refrigerated?"

"No. Just a soda and some dog food I picked up."

I walk over to the sink area and remove the can of dog food and my drink, placing them on the counter. "You keep these?" I hold up the plastic bag.

He shakes his head. "I get as many as I want from the hardware store. Just toss it in the can there." He points to the trashcan at the end of the counter, right near the sliding backdoor.

I throw the bag away and face Farmer who is now stirring the chili with a wooden spoon.

"Another ten minutes and we'll be ready. Other than the uhhh ... Halloween shenanigans, everything else okay at the store?"

"Fine. No customers, save for the three trick o' treaters and the dickhead."

"There's always some boys in town that pull pranks. Need a good whoopin', if you ask me."

"He about got one from me, then he took off."

Farmer's face tells me he's conflicted. Not seriously so, but he's clearly debating something.

"What?" I ask.

"To look at you and not know much about you, I

would've guessed you were being a little over confident there. But something tells me I'd be wrong and that you could've handled him just fine."

He's not wrong. I do have to be careful here. I can tell a deeper inquisition is about to begin. Farmer is an honest, hardworking, red-blooded American. I don't think he would understand the existence of a place like AWT or people like me or Madame K or Amatto. To Farmer, that kind of thing belongs in movies and never in a civilized society.

"I've been through a lot, grew up in tough neighborhoods. I had to learn to defend myself very early or I'd never have survived."

"I don't doubt that. To look in your eyes, it's pretty obvious you've seen things a few things. I don't even know how old you are, Annie, but I'd guess your soul is much older."

"You are probably right on all counts there. Which is I why I'm glad to be here, where life is generally quiet and I can try to move past certain things. I think there's a good person inside of me somewhere. Sometimes, the environment you choose to live in can make all the difference. Wouldn't you agree?"

"I do, for the most part, but some people, it just doesn't matter where they go. Deep down, we are who we are." He puts up his hands. "And I don't mean to suggest anything bad about you, just speaking in generalities here."

"I get what you mean."

"Life has a way of molding us. We're like the moon, cratered and banged up. We started out smooth, but over time, we get dinged up and scarred. It's hard to shake the memory of how we got those scars, no matter where we are."

I give a few nods.

"But hey," Farmer says, "I didn't have you over here to get so serious in the first five minutes. We can at least wait until we've had some pie before we crack open." He winks and turns to stir the chili again. He takes a small taste. "Oh yeah. We're ready now."

"Awesome. I'm starving. You got a can opener so I can open Roadie's food.? Oh, and a plate and a spoon?"

He opens and reaches into a drawer to the right of the stove and pulls out a can opener and three spoons, then opens the cabinet just above that. He removes two large bowls and a plate, placing the bowls on the counter. He turns and hands me the three items I requested.

I thank him and go to work on getting Roadie's dinner ready. He's instantly at my feet as I open the can. I dump the food on the plate and smash it around with the back of the spoon. I put the plate on the floor near the back door and throw the empty can in the trash.

Farmer is using a ladle to serve up the chili. He puts a spoon in each of our bowls and hands one to me.

"Let's eat in the dining room. It's just around to the left. There are napkins and oyster crackers on the table already."

I grab my diet soda bottle and follow him in there.

The dining room is well-lit by an ornate crystal chandelier and is closer in style to the entry of the home. There is lots of original woodwork, long ivory drapes over the three large windows, and in the center of the room, a rectangle six-seater mission-style dining room table, cherry stained and immaculate. There's a fall-themed silk flower centerpiece on the table along with a salt and pepper shaker, a small stack of white paper napkins, and a zipper bag of oyster crackers. Each seat has a burnt orange placemat in front of it too.

We sit at the two seats closest to the doorway coming from the kitchen. Farmer grabs the oyster crackers and shakes some out of the bag onto his chili. He offers them up to me but I shake my head.

Before he starts to eat, Farmer lowers his head slightly, closes his eyes, and I can only assume, says an internal pray. We've talked at the store about my lack of religiosity, so he doesn't bother asking me to join. Out of respect, I wait for him to finish.

When he picks up his spoon, I follow suit and we dig in. I've had dozens of kinds of chili in my day and I will say, this one is pretty damn good. The flavor is perfect, not too spicy with a nice tomato base. Some might refer to this, tongue-in-cheek, as hamburger soup, as it's on the thin side, nonetheless, it tastes great. My favorite is a kind with no beans, thickened with a masa flour and topped with sour cream and cheddar cheese. Either way, I'm having no trouble putting it down.

Without a single word between us, we each quickly empty our bowls.

"I think I was a lot hungrier than I realized," I say before taking a sip of my soda.

"There's plenty more."

"No, no, I'm fine. I horked it down so fast, I better let it settle before considering seconds. I gotta leave room for pie."

"That's a good point. I'll follow your lead." Farmer pushes his bowl away from him. "I sure hope that prankster didn't startle you too much. Boys around here can take things too far sometimes."

I shake my head. "Nah. I don't startle easy. I was more concerned about the door."

"And I appreciate that. I've actually replaced that door four times."

"Four times? Christ! What the hell happened?"

"The first time, nothing. It was just old. The second time was when a car pulled into a parking spot out front and their brakes gave out. Rolled right into the building. Shattered most of the glass, bent the door and some of the structure around it. That was an exciting day. Town really came to together to help us out, cleaning up the mess, securing the store with plywood. It was nice. Small town values. Nothing beats community."

"Wow. That's great."

"Let's see ... the third time, some a-hole threw a brick through one of the windows and the door. Never did figure out who did that. Probably some kids."

"This town is starting to sound a little dangerous. I should probably move." I hold my stern face for four seconds then finally smile.

"Ahhh, you almost had me there. I'll be honest. I'm getting kinda used to having you around. Makes me miss the wife and my girls a little less."

I put my hand on his and give it a few taps. "That's nice of you to say." I pull my hand back and grab my soda for another sip. I wish I could fully reciprocate his feelings, but my life and wherever I happen to be is always fleeting. I have no intentions of going anywhere, and maybe I'll be around for a while, but internally, I still have yet to accept this as a permanent home or anything close to it.

"Well, certainly your daughters visit from time to time, right?"

"When they can. Busy lives. And since they don't live nearby, it's not exactly like they can just drive over."

"Will they come for the holidays at all?"

"Doubtful."

I can tell he wants to change the subject, so I oblige.

"So, what happened the fourth time you replaced the door?"

"That was just last year ... and a doozy. We had a terrible storm roll through here. This was like, seventeen months ago now. There were tornados, which are pretty rare here. An F2 hit a nearby county. We just got ridiculously high winds. Quite a bit of damage around town. A little corner of the roof got torn off the IGA. Ummm, you know the little white awning that's over our door?"

I nod. "I do."

"Well, that sucker snapped right off the bolts holding it to the building, and with only a small metal strap still connected, it came a swinging down and slammed right into the door. There wasn't a piece of glass bigger than a pea on the ground. Completely shattered."

"I bet the sound of that was tremendous. Make you pee your pants."

"Oh yeah. Luckily, I was in the back of the store when it happened. We don't have a basement over there, so I was taking cover in the office, which doesn't have any windows. No one was hurt in town, so it turned out okay."

"That's good. I've never experienced a tornado. Some hurricanes, sure, a little nor'easter from time to time, of course, but no twisters. I'll pass on that. I've seen the Bill Paxton movie."

"Extreme weather does one thing really well," Farmer says then pauses.

"Oh yeah, what's that?"

"It forces us to take stock in our lives."

"I've never really thought of it like that, but I suppose you're right."

"On most days, we just walk through life, trying to get from one day to the next, thinking about what we have to gain from moving forward. But when we're facing down a tornado ... or a hurricane, suddenly our thoughts shift and we start to realize what we have to lose. Our lives, our families," he pauses and looks over to Roadie and then around the room, "our pets and our homes. As terrible as these events are, they sure do help to bring us back to the important things. During that storm, sitting back in the office, even though I rarely see them, all I could think about was Cameron and Wendy."

Farmer looks away from me slightly. The fact he doesn't get to see his family very often clearly affects him more than he lets on. He is normally so even-keeled, stoic in most cases, so seeing him like this makes me appreciate him even more.

I doubt he opens up like this to anyone else, so I should be honored. I suppose I am. And while I'm happy to play the part of confidant and friend to Farmer, what he really needs to do is make more of an effort to stay connected to his actual daughters. I'm only now beginning to remember and learn the value of family for myself.

I can only imagine having a father I could call when I need advice, to share in my important life events, or just to chat about whatever interests we might share. My only adult guardian was Rosemary, and that wasn't exactly a nurturing, parental relationship. She was more like a work supervisor. The bad side of the world raised me, the anger, the fear, the hard reality of survival. I had no family. People to me were either useful in my pursuits or not, enemies or not.

I decide to open up a little, despite the risk to us both.

"We all take things for granted. Despite the difficulties you experience, I envy you."

"Oh?" He looks back to me.

"Yes. I've never really had a family. My parents disappeared when I was very young. I barely even remember them. I'd kill to even have the option of calling up my dad just to say hi."

"What happened, if you don't mind me asking?"

I decide to keep it vague. "No one knows. They were never found and I was raised in the foster system, never adopted." The Leer family instantly comes to mind. They are family to me, of sorts. "I'm realizing in this very moment that I've spent most of my life wanting a family, a deeper connection to people, but my anger and bitterness over losing my parents left me pushing people away. I guess, subconsciously, I wouldn't allow myself to be in a situation where I could lose people again."

Wow. That's a hell of a breakthrough. I hope Dina, analyzing from the great beyond, is nodding and smiling at her work still in motion.

"I'm really sorry you had to go through that. I can't even imagine the pain that would bring a child. I think this calls for pie." Farmer rises from his chair. I try to follow suit but he stops me. "I got it. You relax. If I make coffee, will you drink any?"

"Thank you. Yes."

"Big shot of cream, right?"

"You got it."

"Be right back."

He leaves the dining room and returns to the kitchen.

I turn in my seat and scratch Roadie's chin, then pet him on the head.

"You probably need to go outside." I get up and walk to the front door, opening it. Roadie is right behind me. "Go on. Go potty."

Roadie runs by me and is off the porch. As I stand here watching him rummage around the yard, I think about my relationship with Farmer, his surrogate father to my surrogate daughter. Lucky coincidence for us both. The independent streak in me, the lowlife in me, wants to run far away from this, but the practical human side of me wants to dive right in and let it evolve as it may. Would it be so bad to have a reliable and kind father figure in my life, to allow some external guidance, to depend on someone else? To do so might open the door to more pain and abandonment. I've already managed to put myself in a position where I can't be a part of the Leer's lives anymore. I've suffered betrayal at the hands of a Kill Team member and the company I work for is hunting me, which resulted in the death of Dina, and for that I will likely be killed if they find me. To put a nice little bow on top of all that mess, I lost my dear friend Sake Tom. Risk versus reward. Could I bear it should the trend continue? I don't know if I can answer that.

Farmer finds me on the porch, my face no doubt sharing my internal strife.

"Your body is here but your eyes tell me you're miles away," he says.

"Oh, just trying to reconcile a few things. Some choices are just so fuckin' hard. Fear of the unknown is going to give me a damn heart attack. And the past, yuck. Moving on can be so difficult." I lean over and tap my thighs to call Roadie up to the porch. He complies.

"From my experience, the things we fear to do, when we finally do them, are often far less of a big deal than we imagined. Living with regret and doubt is probably worse. Take a leap."

"If only it were that simple."

"That's my point. In hindsight, it almost always is. Hell, I would have never met Evelyn if I hadn't put aside my fear and just jumped in, literally. We met at a public pool in the town we grew up. I jumped in the water and splashed the hell out of her as she sat by the edge of the pool. She was upset, initially, but it worked as the icebreaker I hoped it would. I pondered going over to talk to her every Saturday that summer before I finally did. In the end, my fears were completely unfounded."

"I hear ya, and you're right." I don't tell him of the real risks to his life and my own that might come with allowing him to be too close to me. We aren't there yet. Someday, maybe. For now, I'll play the part of receptive daughter.

"As for the past," he says, "best just face it. There's a festering monster that lives back there, and if you don't kill it, the damn thing will attack you when you least expect it."

"This monster might just kill *me*." I know he will automatically assume I mean a past boyfriend, husband, or whatever, but the monster I'm running from is a trained hunter with a fucking attitude problem of the highest order. I'll let Farmer keep his illusions for now.

"Well, hopefully, it won't come to that. The solution is still the same, it's just more delicate. Then again, I'm just an old man who doesn't really know anything, not about what you're going through. Trust your instincts. If they tell you to run, then run."

"My instincts are often all I have."

"You okay if we enjoy our dessert and coffee in the kitchen? I need to stand. Been sitting most of the day."

"Sure."

I usher Roadie past us and back into the house. I'm right behind with Farmer in tow.

"Thanks for inviting me over. It's been ... good."

"You're welcome here any time you like. I should probably be monitored from time to time anyway. When I get bored, I usually get out the power tools, generally the most dangerous saws and the like. I've been told I'm accident prone ... but I've still got all my digits, so I don't know how accurate that theory is."

"I will keep that in mind." Then I add in a deep but playful monster voice, "Now feed me pie."

24

November arrives today with an expected high of sixty-four degrees and I ain't hating that. Tomorrow, Sunday, will be about the same. I'm on my way to work now but I plan on spending some time outside tomorrow just enjoying the warmth of the southwest breeze, maybe relaxing by the creek while listening to a podcast and playing fetch with Roadie.

I'm settling into a nice routine with work, with Roadie, with the cabin. I'm having a hard time deciding what to do with the cabin as far as remodeling is concerned. I mean, I know what needs to be done but I just don't know if this cabin is where I should invest my time and money. It's crossed my mind more than a few times that perhaps I should just rent a duplex or an apartment. I might be a little safer in an environment where there are more people around, as compared to the cabin where if I didn't leave the house for days, I might not see another human being.

The flip side is that the isolation is great too, especially considering I'm likely being hunted and I don't want others to get caught in the crossfire, but should they find me, my current living situation presents too many challenges to overcome. Living in a crowded area could be the difference between living and dying. Not that true professionals will let anything get in their way once they have a mission to kill, but I sure as fuck don't want to make it easy.

One way or another, I'll have to make a decision soon. I love the small town living I've fallen into here in Burton, the people in particular, but there's a huge part of me that says being in a big city will give me a longer shelf life, and right now, I don't feel anywhere near my expiration date.

Perhaps a complete change in environment is what I need. Something like Texas or California. How does one go about deciding something like this, moving somewhere you've never lived before where you don't know anyone? I've never had trouble in the past switching my place of residence. It's always been something I've had no choice but to do, so I see it as a common and necessary part of life. This situation would be different. Moving frequently around the Baltimore area for nearly a decade is not the same as traveling two thousand miles where the people, the food, and the weather are different. I have no doubt that I can adapt and thrive but that doesn't relieve any anxiety that swirls around the idea. Maybe if I took a trip to some of the cities, that might help me decide. That's not a bad thought.

As I drive, I glance down and see that I need to stop and get gas. Just up ahead is the only station in Burton, so I pull in to fill up.

There are four pumps, two on the inner part of the canopy, two on the outer. There's a rusty brown pickup truck at one of the inner spots, so I pull next to the first of the outer ones.

I look over to Roadie who is sitting comfortably in the passenger seat. "Stay put. I gotta get gas. I'll be right back."

I hop out of the car and walk around to the passenger side to begin pumping gas. As I start, I happen to look over to the truck on the opposite side, diagonal from me. There's a bunch of random crap in the bed – firewood, a few bundles of rebar, two large coolers, but the thing that really catches my attention is a silken black hood with a scary white face on it, the exact one worn by the prankster from Halloween night.

In my training and experience, coincidence is rarely just that. As small as Burton and the surrounding county are, it seems highly unlikely there would be two people with that exact same mask from this Halloween. I can feel myself starting to get pissed off. The problem is, I don't know what I can do about it now. I can't call the cops. I'd rather not involve Farmer. I could just walk away and do nothing. I could also confront this asshole. I have no idea how that might end. I'm trying to be a ghost here. Unwanted attention is not my friend. Damn it, Josey! Pump your gas and walk away. Just walk ... the fuck ... away.

A couple of guys emerge from the gas station store and head right for the rusty truck. They're both wearing filthy blue jeans. One has a thin, camo jacket on and well-worn brown boots. The other has on a black hoodie and black work boots that are so worn out, the toes have become slightly detached from the soles and are curling up some. They're both under six feet tall but taller than me, and the one in the hoodie is probably thirty pounds overweight.

I finish pumping, put the nozzle away, and secure my gas cap. As I turn to go in to pay, the guys have both positioned themselves near the rear of their truck, half facing the truck, half facing me. They're trying not to be obvious that they're discussing me, and if I wasn't already paying attention I might not even notice. In my head, I wasn't going to confront them, but now it looks like I won't have a choice.

They creep closer, the one in the camo staying slightly behind the pumps, the one in the black hoodie more confidently stepping right up to me, and in fact, blocking my way so that I'd have to step around him.

"Excuse me," I say with a sarcastic smile.

"I've seen you around here before," he says.

"Congratulations. You have working eyes." I take a step to my right. He follows suit.

"You got a smart mouth."

"Look, dickhead, I'm going to be late for work and I don't have time for games with little boys. Now step aside." My scowl should be telling him that I'm not playing around, but I can guarantee a woman has never spoken to him like this, so he's not going to get the message.

He grabs my left wrist, not too hard though, and I snap it away easily.

Before he can even get another word out of his filthy mouth, with my left hand I grab his left wrist, spin him around to where he's facing his friend, twist his arm just enough to hurt, then apply pressure to his shoulder in just the right place to immobilize him. He tries to wiggle out but the pain halts his movement. He squelches in agony.

Camo boy steps out from behind the pump. Roadie growls.

I look the guy square in the eyes. "Don't you take one more fucking step or I'm going to snap your buddy's arm out of the socket and break his wrist. You'll be opening his ketchup bottles for the next three months."

He takes me seriously and holds firm.

"Let me go you fuckin' bitch," my prisoner squeaks like a baby mouse. His eyes are watering, his face red.

Roadie barks twice.

"I agree, Roadie. That is definitely no way to talk to a lady." I turn his wrist a tiny fraction and it forces him to his knees. He yelps.

"Now, I know it was one of you assholes that scratched the door of the hardware store on Halloween night, but I'm going to give you a pass in exchange for never seeing your faces around here again. I don't care why you're here, where you came from, or where you go. I just don't want you here. If I see your ugly fucking faces again, this," I stop to twist his arm a little more, "will seem like child's play compared to what I will do to you. Got it?"

The camo asshole nods vigorously but I don' hear a peep from my prisoner, so I get louder. "GOT IT?"

He nods once and follows it with a baby voiced yes.

"Good." I release his arm and throw him off to the side. He collapses to the ground. "Have a lovely rest of your day."

I walk to the gas station door to find the cashier standing there holding the door open. He's an older man, maybe in his sixties. Looks like a guy who smokes three packs a day and at the end of the workweek comes home with a twenty-four pack of Busch for the weekend.

"Everything okay, ma'am?"

I nod. "Just a slight disagreement about Halloween night behavior and how not to treat a woman. We resolved it." I turn to find camo guy trying to help up his friend but getting slapped away. I turn back and walk past the cashier and into the store.

"Ok then," the cashier says. He returns to his place behind the register.

I grab a diet cola from one of the freestanding coolers near the front of the store and go to pay.

"I don't think those boys are from around here."

"We won't be seeing them again." I smile.

"Just the gas and the soda then?"

"Yep."

He rings me up. "That'll be twenty-two eighteen."

I pay with a twenty and a five. He hands me the change and I just stuff it into my front right pocket.

"Thanks." I nod and leave the store.

The rusty pickup truck is gone. I seem to attract the worst assholes in any quadrant I happen to be in. Been like that most of my life. Luckily for me, I can handle myself. Only difference today is that I carry guns. Thinking about that, I actually wouldn't mind having a stun gun again. I could never go back to one exclusively, my life is just too dangerous now, but when dealing with local idiots like I just did, it might be better. I can't go around shooting people. Well, I mean, I could, but I'd never be able to settle down anywhere. I can't have that.

I get in the car and rub Roadie's chin. "You got good instincts, boy. But we gotta get to work."

I start the car and get on the road. As I drive, I keep playing the incident in my head. I realize how calm I am in those situations. I've been able to handle myself long before my days at AWT, but now, my heart rate never even elevated during the gas station encounter. There's something comforting about that but also unnerving. I don't think I want a life like that, one where I'm always maneuvering out of tricky situations, hurting people, killing some. My taste for it appears to be subsiding. I just want to go to work, be helpful, and chill for a while.

I can see there's a nature versus nurture thing happening for me. Is it in my blood to live on the darker side of life, to be right in the middle of whatever struggles are happening around me, to be the fixer? Or is this all my training, my environment, a cumulation of my life's circumstances? Dina would have some insight. Tom would too. Unfortunately, I don't have either one of them to bounce my crazy off of. Damn it. I'm sure Farmer would have some sage advice but I don't think he's ready for the paid assassin conversation. Time will tell, I suppose.

25

Sunday Afternoon

The little creek behind the cabin has about three inches of water trickling through it. Roadie loves it. He runs adjacent to the water until he spots a frog. He'll stop, stalk his prey almost like a damn cat, then pounce with a splash into the water and always come up with nothing. Not the greatest hunter, this one, but he's too cute when he tries.

Work yesterday was mostly boring. Farmer and I were both present. I never mentioned the gas station incident as I don't want him worrying about me. I spent most of the shift cleaning, organizing, and preparing to shift the store from fall to winter inventory. A few guys came in for lawn bags, one for a toilet tank repair kit. A woman came in right when we opened looking for plumbing supplies related to a leaky kitchen sink. Her speaker phone conversations with her husband were hilarious.

"They don't have a plastic black pipe shaped like a J," the woman said.

"Well, that's what I need," the man said.

"What if you took a U pipe and added a straight one?

Then it becomes a J."

"Can you just show Farmer the pictures we took? Jesus woman."

"I can figure this out. I'm not an idiot."

"I never said that. I just don't wanna be under this damn sink all day."

"Fine. I just want this fixed so I can run the dishwasher again."

They had gone on for five full minutes before that part. When she finally asked for assistance, Farmer was able to help her out in a matter of about ninety seconds. Their bickering put me in a good mood though.

Today, I'm just enjoying a warm, peaceful day watching Roadie play, sipping on a coffee. I bought one of the camping chairs from the hardware store made from pipe and canvas that folds up for easy transport. The cup holder sold me. I placed the chair about ten feet from the water's edge. Sitting here, I can't help but think about how cool it would be to do a firepit, cook some hotdogs, roast some marshmallows, maybe even invite Farmer, Bernard, Jake, and Becky over. Good time of year for that sort of thing.

I look over to my right and see Roadie with his nose at the ground, sniffing around like he's found something interesting. Maybe one day he'll get that frog.

I take a sip of coffee and look back to find Roadie unconsciously making his way back toward the cabin. I stare at the ground where he was a minute ago and something draws my attention. The soil in that area is moist and soft, and there are impressions much like when a person steps in mud. They are too big and deep to be from Roadie. I haven't stepped in that area today and they look fresh. I try to ignore it but my instincts and training kick in.

I rise from my chair and slowly make my way to the spot on the ground. Roadie barks once from somewhere near the cabin but I pay no attention. I'm locked in on the dirt impressions. They are not clean enough to know for sure, as they overlap, but they look big enough to be men's boots, two sets, one behind and slightly crossing over the other. They seem to originate from across the creek. They lead to my cabin.

Roadie barks again. Then again.

I turn to find him near the kitchen side porch. I follow the footprints to where Roadie is investigating.

"What do you smell, Roadie?"

He growls and is fixated on something near the feet of the little charcoal grill.

I reach down and pick up a crushed beer can. I know for a fact that wasn't there before. I smell the opening and shake some of the moisture out. It's fresh enough to know that it hasn't been there more than a day or two.

My thoughts gravitate toward the two guys from the gas station. And gravitate seems to be a good word here, as once again, negative attention anywhere near me almost always ends up falling to me. I was fully intent on letting that masked vandal slide, but they approached me and I was forced to deal with them against my will.

Now, it appears they may be stalking me, probably to get even for embarrassing them. Or, it could have been a couple of locals hiking through the woods, just following the creek. Maybe they were curious about the cabin, that quite frankly, still looks somewhat abandoned from the outside. Another possibility, though remote, is that someone from AWT is on to me. The beer can eliminates that choice. No one at AWT would be that careless. Unless the can is a plant to make me believe it's locals. That would actually be clever. My gut says it was the Halloween pranksters. I'm anxious now, on edge. I left my old life behind so I could find a new way to exist, and yet...

I get a little tingle down my spine knowing that someone was creeping around the property, possibly while I slept. Apparently, they were just quiet enough not to alarm the dog. Had they stepped on the creaky front porch, Roadie would have noticed.

I look down at Roadie, thankful he found me. I crouch down and rub his face, then pat his back. "You're such a good boy. Thank you for looking out for me. I'm a lucky girl." I rise back up.

I start to think about the extra precautions I need to take. I already have loaded weapons in the cabin. I'll double up on those and have them at the ready.

Without high speed internet, I can't exactly throw up a few cloud cams. That's a bummer.

I could setup a perimeter alert system on the property but I'm too damn lazy for that.

I'm actually off work today, Monday, and Tuesday, so I could do a good ol' fashioned recon job, stake out the property myself and catch these fuckers in the act. Almost sounds like fun, but lying in the bush for two days, pissing and shitting in a hole, eating protein bars and jerky, and having nothing but water to drink sounds too much like the life I'm trying to escape. I'd prefer to let that muscle atrophy.

I guess I'll just sit in bed, watching TV, surrounded by a few dozen fully loaded, high-powered guns, waiting for my stalkers to show up so I can scare them so bad they'll never fuck with a tiny woman again. Yeah. That's a winner right there.

26

My nerves are set to high potential conflict levels. Once I found the footprints and the beer can, I've only been able to have some tea and water to drink. No food. Don't get me wrong, I'm not scared, not really even worried, but when I'm on the verge of a battle or a mission, I find it hard to eat. This hasn't always been the case. When I first started at AWT, I had no problem shoving down a bunch of cheeseburgers right before nailing my target. A few months before the Kill Team began what would become their final mission, the one in Texas, my appetite suddenly changed. I don't think I would call it butterflies, but maybe that's what it is.

I can tell you what Dina would say. She'd be like, "You're getting nervous because this job has become important to you and so the stakes are now higher. That changes how a person handles the work, their preparation, their emotional state, everything. Even the filter by which an assassin views the world evolves as their level of dedication evolves."

And of course, my response would be the usual brushing off of the idea I actually cared, and that nothing has changed as far as my commitment, followed by my famous, wide-eyed, blank stare of incredulous boredom.

But she could always see through my bravado, and she

knew that her wisdom got through to me, whether I ever showed it or not. I can admit now that I took her for granted. Luckily or unluckily, depending on one's viewpoint, her voice seems to be haunting me from beyond the grave.

Something interesting just popped into my head though, an idea that's never once crossed my mind. Perhaps being an assassin was never the right path for me. I've always had a knack for understanding people, their motivations, their behavior. Maybe, with the right schooling and training, being the next Dina was my destiny all along. But shit, who am I kidding. My days at AWT are long gone. And school. That's a laugh. Me, Josey Baldwin, sitting in a classroom all day, studying textbooks, taking exams, writing essays, not punching people in the face or killing anyone. That seems about as far-fetched as me suddenly deciding to go away to become a nun. Ha! No fucking way, on both counts.

Earlier today, I retraced the footprints away from the cabin, along the creek, over the creek, through the woods a little way, and eventually to a dirt road just off of Route 34. There I found exactly what I expected, and that was the tire tracks of a large pickup truck. There wasn't much I could do at that moment except return home and prepare for the worst.

I laid out all my weapons on the kitchen table and on the kitchen counters. I took the time to disassemble some and clean them thoroughly. Once I finished that step, I loaded the ones I wanted to keep out and stored away the rest.

I kept out three large rifles, two of which have scopes and are long range, and the other a more practical household .22 that anyone might find at a sporting gear store. I keep that one next to the door in my bedroom.

I also have seven handguns of varying calibers. I'll keep two on my person, three somewhere in the bedroom, one in a kitchen drawer, and the last one hidden somewhere by the couch. This will give me options should I need to start improvising. I'll have a few blades strapped on too for any fierce hand-to-hand combat that might arise. With Roadie by my side, I feel totally prepared.

Now, it's after eleven p.m. and I'm in bed pretending to be asleep while Roadie snores at my feet. I keep closing my eyes and snapping them back open. I can't stop yawning either. This is going to be a long night.

I open my eyes. I had fallen asleep sitting up in bed with my head tipped too far back. Now my neck hurts. I tilt my head from side to side, slowly, to stretch the muscles. It doesn't help much. My eyes quickly adjust to the dark and I can tell Roadie is no longer in the room. I turn my ear toward the door and listen. My heart pumps a tad faster at the sound of his low growl.

I hop from the bed, two knives and a pistol already strapped on, and grab the silver 9mm with the black grip sitting on my nightstand.

I leave the bedroom and find Roadie crouched down on the living room floor, about ten feet from the front door.

"Good boy," I say as I pass him.

When I get there, I put my ear to the door and listen. I don't hear anything. I turn the deadbolt as quietly as I can, release the knob lock, and carefully twist the knob and pull the door open about three inches. With no outdoor lights on, it's hard to see, but in the pale light of the crescent moon, I can make out the white and tan shape of a doe thirty feet out, just near the road.

My stomach drops. My shoulder tension releases. Roadie's growling intensifies. I'm sure he'd love for me to open the door so he can chase off the deer but I'm too tired now to wait for him to finally return after a ten-minute chase.

With one hand still on the doorknob, I turn toward him and tell him to hush. He ignores me and lets out consecutive barks instead.

"You shit. Calm down. Not tonight."

I begin to turn back around when suddenly my wrist wrenches and the door flies open. I have no choice but to release the knob. I bring up my right hand to point my gun but it's too late. Someone is on me and we are on the ground in a flash. I lose my grip on the gun and it launches away from me toward the couch. Roadie is angry barking right next to us. I sense a second person come through the door. He shuts it behind him.

The man near the door has a flashlight. I can see the beam bouncing around the room.

Roadie barks incessantly.

"Shut that fucking dog up!" screams the guy on top of me. He weighs about eighty to a hundred pounds more than me, so my attempts to buck him off are ineffective. He's also managed to pin my arms to the floor with a tight grip on my wrists.

"You touch my fuckin' dog, I'll kill you both," I snarl.

He lets go of my left wrist and slaps me hard across the face.

I wince but don't make a noise. He's definitely not playing around. What he doesn't know is that with my hand free, I am able to reach down and secure one of my knives. It's a Japanese made hunting knife with a five-inch blade and a brown leather wrapped handle.

I jam the blade right into his love handle.

He immediately releases my other hand, arching his back as he looks toward the ceiling. He screams before sliding sideways in the direction of the living room and off of me.

I roll toward the kitchen and jump to my feet just as the guy with the flashlight finds the switch and turns on the kitchen light. I can see now these assholes are indeed the same ones from the gas station. The guy holding the flashlight is the more passive camo guy. The one I stabbed is still wearing the black hoodie from the other day.

Surprisingly, Roadie, though still barking, has not attacked.

"Roadie, quiet!" I yell. He stops barking and switches to a guttural growl. His head is low and he looks ready to attack. Maybe he is waiting for a command from me.

"You fucking stabbed me," the guy on the ground blubbers out. "I can't believe you fucking stabbed me."

I snatch the small pistol from around my ankle and point it in rotation between the two of them.

I can see a gun tucked behind the waist of camo guy's pants but he hasn't pulled it. Amateur. I don't see an obvious weapon on the guy on the ground. I assume he has something.

"Both of you, don't move or I'll shoot you in the face." I look over briefly to the bleeder. "And you jumped me. I was defending myself you idiot."

"We were just having some fun." He's trying to hold the wound closed by applying pressure but the blood keeps pooling into his hand. He won't make it much longer without medical attention. He's already turned a shade whiter. I can see in his eyes he's suddenly aware that his life is on a short clock. "I think ... I think ... I might be dying. Jesus, Rodney. Help me out here." He falls awkwardly to his side.

Rodney is frozen in fear. He can't even look at his friend who is now white as a sheet and covered in blood. His eyes stay locked on me, the one with the gun pointed at his face.

"I know what you're thinking, Rodney. Can I pull my gun and get off a shot before this bitch puts a hole in me? The answer is no, Rodney. You cannot. I happen to be expertly trained in firearms. I could put a bullet straight up your nose from this range. Believe it."

I'm not quite that good, but he doesn't know that.

From the guy on the floor, "She's lying. Shoot that bitch." His words eek out, his breathing labored.

I glance over and point the gun briefly. "Shut the fuck up dummy. We've already established your decision-making skills are poor, at best."

I'm back on Rodney. I don't like what I see. I can tell he's scheming. I lock eyes with him and give him two deliberate, slow head shakes. The beam from the flashlight is wobbly. His hands are trembling.

"Rod...neeeeeeey. Your buddy here is going to be dead in about two minutes but you don't have to be. Think about it."

Roadie barks once, takes a step closer to me, and returns

to growling after I give him a sour look.

In the split second I looked down to Roadie, Rodney has decided to pull the gun. Damn it. I was hoping we could finish this a different way.

"You ... you drop that gun." His hands are shaking even more than they were a minute ago. Roadie barks twice when Rodney stops talking.

"I can't do that, Rodney."

With a sudden burst of confidence, Rodney demands, "Drop that gun and help Jake. If he dies, so do you."

"It's too late for him." I take a millisecond glance to Jake. He's not moving at all. He's likely already dead.

I have a few choices running through my head here. I could just preemptively take Rodney out and avoid any chance of getting shot myself. I could dive further into the kitchen, flipping over the table to use as a barricade and get into a shootout. Or I could continue trying to talk him down. Truth is, I'm exhausted and I'm already thinking about how I'm going to deal with the potential aftermath of all this.

I have one dead body to my right, and if Rodney doesn't stop now, I'm going to have two on my hands. There's not much difference in dealing with one or two, so I make a decision to put an end to the situation.

"Time's up, Rodney. I'm giving you to the count of three, and if you don't drop that gun, you're going to join Jake on the floor."

Roadie can sense an impending escalation. He starts to bark repeatedly.

I give Rodney a few seconds to respond. He chooses not to.

"One."

I count three seconds in my head. I can tell he's thinking but has doubts.

"Shut that fuckin' dog up! I can't stand it anymore."

"Roadie! Stop!"

He ignores me. If I'm being honest, he's starting to annoy me too. In the small space of the cabin, his bark is ear-piercing.

I go on, "Two."

"You shoot me, you're dead too," Rodney says.

"Nope. Just you, Rodney. Just you."

"Uhhh ... that fuckin' dog needs to be quiet." He drops the flashlight. The clanks startles Roadie but he keeps barking. Rodney rubs his upper thigh with his now free hand but he keeps the gun on me. His agitation level is maxed out. I don't have much time.

"Last chance. Please drop the gun and we can both walk outta here." I know it's a lie as I have no choice but to put him down now.

"Shut him up! I can't think. I can't think."

I see my opportunity and don't even bother to finish the countdown.

I aim for the torso as my training tells me. That way he'll buckle and then I can edge closer and finish him off.

I fire two shots. He tries to move at the last moment but both bullets hit him. As he bends forward, he gets off one shot that misses to my right. There's a yelp. Suddenly, there is no gunfire, no barking, no talking.

I peek down at Roadie and find him down on his side, a small pool of blood spreading from underneath him. I lose my shit, my mind going blank with white, hot fury.

I charge Rodney and slam him into the front door. I throw my free arm around him as best I can and manage to muscle him to the floor. I get tripped up on his feet and land on him. I square myself to him, and with my gun two inches from his face, I empty the clip. The splatter of flesh, blood, and bone is horrifying. At this point, I doubt he could even be identified with dental records.

I fall backward off him and onto my butt. I use leg power to slide myself away from him. I twist around toward Roadie but I can't bear to look at him. My gun falls to the floor and I use my left hand to broadly wipe Rodney off my face. I sit on the floor, the anger subsiding, and replacing it is the feeling of being in a vast, hollow, dark space where emotions don't exist and all time slips quickly into a black hole.

27

I'm on the couch, blood still on my face and my hands, splattered all over my clothes. The bodies are right where I left them, but out of respect, and maybe because I just can't look at him without bawling, I covered Roadie up with a sheet.

The self-loathing is strong with me right now. All I can think about is the fact that everyone that comes near me ends up hurt or dead. And now it appears that also translates to animals. If there is such a thing as the opposite of the Midas touch, I think I have it, like a highly contagious virus. Get anywhere close to me and go ahead and start counting down the days of your life. Rather than risk one more life, perhaps the best thing I could do is off myself. I see my gun on the floor over near the kitchen, the one I used to dispatch Rodney. I envision myself walking over to get it, pointing it under my chin toward the center-mass of my head, and bang.

The local authorities would never figure out what happened in this cabin. It would make absolutely no sense. We'd be talked about for years and years. Fortunately, I'm out of the murderous trance I fell into after last night's fall from grace, and I just don't have the constitution for suicide. Whether I end up dead by the hands of someone at AWT, that is still to be determined, but it appears I have no choice now but to face my past in order to decide if I have a future. One thing I know for certain is that more blood is going to be spilled.

I can't decide if I'm going to clean this place up or burn it down and leave. This cabin is part of Tom's legacy for me and I hate to just destroy it, but once I leave, I'll never see it again, so I suppose it doesn't matter much.

Figuring out how to say goodbye to Farmer is a bigger problem. He trusted me, let me into his life, and treated me like family. Now I have to abandon him. I'll write him a note explaining that it was time to move on. I've not shared much with him about my family, other than my parents went missing, so I'll just make up a story about a half-sister in the Pacific Northwest that is willing to take me in and give me a fresh start, far away from all my troubles. I don't know if he'll buy it, but like the cabin, I'll likely never see him again. When it's discovered the cabin is burned down and I mysteriously ran away, suspicions will forever be too high for me to ever return.

The two idiots I had to dispatch last night won't be missed. I have no idea where they even came from or what they were doing around these parts. Doesn't matter now. They're dead. I'm not. I'll make sure there is nothing left of their bodies to discover and find some way to dispose of their truck.

I will, however, give Roadie a proper burial near the creek. In our short time together, he was friendly, loyal, and one of the more positive things to come into my life in a while. He deserves nothing less.

Tiny bits of an idea float through my head, finally coalescing into a full plan. If I'm going to have a chance against Madame K, I need her on my turf. How I get the woman out of her element is going to be the tough part. I need to call Ollie. I need to clean myself up and get my stuff into the car. I need to bury and burn as required to cleanse the scene. I need to end this shit once and for all.

I rise from the couch and head to the bathroom. When I catch a glimpse of my face, the blood smear left by my hand, the clumps in my hair, it angers me. I didn't want this yet it happened just the same. I face the mirror directly, a stern and scorned woman staring back. Annie died last night. Josey has been resurrected. That much is clear. An indelible truth creeps forward and takes hold. Josey Baldwin is a killer and death will always surround her.

There are two options. Embrace the lifestyle of a contract killer, for which there seems to be no escape, and at least in that capacity, be able to exercise some modicum of control. Or continually try to live the lie of normality with one foot constantly in and one foot out, never getting to fully exist in one world or the other. In both choices, it appears people will die and people will get hurt. I'm tired of feeling false and disconnected from myself, so clearly there isn't a real choice at all. This person staring back at me, the kid who never had a chance to be normal, the teenager who found a way through crime to survive on the harsh streets of Baltimore, the adult who kills people.

I shower and put on a freshly laundered all-black outfit. I leave the disgusting old rags, shoes included, on the bathroom floor. They'll burn with the rest of this place. I go to the bed and sit on the edge to lace up the black boots, always the last thing to do right before grabbing the weapons.

When done, I sift through the nightstand. From inside the drawer I pull the cell phone I use to contact Ollie. I almost tossed that fucker into a number of different bodies of water over the last couple of weeks, but luckily, I didn't. The time has come for me to call in a favor and put into motion my plan to draw out the monster.

I dial and put the phone to my ear.

"Can you talk?" I ask with a firm staccato.

"Hang on," Ollie responds.

There's some rustling around and then I hear three consecutive beeps.

"I can now. We have about three minutes."

"I need to deal with Madame K. I want her to come to me. I have no chance on her turf." Hearing my tone, I can't help but compare myself to a robot assassin, devoid of emotion.

"I have to admit, I didn't think I'd ever hear from you again, but I'm glad you called."

"Time is short, so let's skip the pleasantries. I need you to send a message to Madame K. After that, I need her to come to me. The problem is, I don't know what I can do to make that happen. Any thoughts?"

"The Dean told me about a plan she concocted that would essentially dismantle the Kill Academy, at least by appearances, and it could drive Madame K away from here ... with the right motivations. A threatening message from you might do the trick, in conjunction with the Dean's plan, I'm almost certain she'd go to you."

"How fast can we move on this?"

"I need to talk to the Dean first, but if I had to guess, we could set this thing in motion within two to three days, with the final part of getting her away from here happening a day or so after that."

"Okay. Do it. Call me back with the details. I need a few days to prepare anyway."

"Is everything okay? I'm no Dina, but I don't need a degree in psychology to know that tone in your voice."

"No, everything is not okay. It's just time to put an end this shit. Call me with the plan. Goodbye."

I hang up the phone and place it on top of the nightstand. I think about the work left for me to do before I can set this place ablaze and ride off to whatever fate has in store for me. At least I don't have to clean up all the blood and body parts. I'll get some acid to dissolve the bodies. The fire will do the rest.

Ollie mentioning Dina reminds me of one of the journal entries I read recently. She made an observation about assassins that seems to fit my situation all too perfectly.

After a few recent sessions with Ridge, Amatto, Gustav, and Maisie, I've come to realize how profoundly this work changes a person. To be in this business, a person must have the preexisting condition I call darkly damage. An assassin's life before taking on such work is often filled with dire circumstances, a rough upbringing with varying degrees of abuse, and no shortage of truly horrific life and death events.

This darkly damage sets the perfect groundwork but that is not to say the assassin doesn't evolve further. The discipline, the structure, and the training we provide here often takes their fractured, wild minds to a more focused place where they can channel their rage and self-doubt.

The more interesting aspect, however, is that there seems to be no going back. Once they are acclimated to this lifestyle, history suggests they are here for life, or more accurately I suppose, here until they die. If there is a law of attraction, being an assassin and having that past darkly damage seems to encapsulate them in a never-ending stream of danger.

I tend to see this phenomenon as something close to the conception of a human life. One chromosome represents the life of an assassin and everything that comes with it. The other chromosome has their past history, their personality, and their nature. Each part is its own entity, but once they come together, they create an entirely new organism, equal parts of the original, yet now something wholly new. This new thing can be nurtured, it can evolve, but it cannot escape where it came from, nor can it change what it now is.

The instinct to act, to kill, and to survive never subsides, not once the chromosomes are joined. The point of all this being - once the path is chosen, it is a choice that cannot be undone.

Dina's words confirm exactly what I have come to realize. There is no escaping who I am. My attempt to go back in time and erase my past by living a completely new life backfired in the most spectacular way. If I ever want to find a peace in my mind and heart, I will have to embrace who I am. If I can't find a way to do that, I might as well be dead.

With any luck, in a few short days I'll be facing down my past. I don't feel confident I'll even make it out alive, but it almost doesn't matter. If I die, I'll do so with the knowledge I stood up, faced the situation, and did so being my true self.

Part III
My Future

28

AWT Headquarters

The atmosphere around AWT has shifted. The once tense, distrustful, and murderous environment has reverted to the usual balance of authority, respect, and cautious edge it once had before the likes of Josey Baldwin. At least on the surface.

With no Kill Team in place and no recruits in the building, Marty and Tisha, lead Tech Ops, spend most of their time upgrading various systems and hardware throughout AWT and helping out the veteran assassins with their missions.

After Dina's funeral, Vick took a role assisting Greg as the resident firearms and weapons expert and trainer. They test all the new equipment that comes from the engineers of AWT, and they've even started to submit some concept stuff of their own. Vick is still wheelchair bound with no use of his legs but holds out hope that with emerging technologies in the field of spinal nerve regeneration using stem cells, he'll one day walk again.

Ollie and Li Xia have taken over Dina's role as recruiter while they train and acclimate the newest addition to their team, Dr. Edmond Chardy.

Dr. Chardy came to the United States as an infant when his parents emigrated from Lyon, France. He earned his doctorate of Philosophy of Psychology with a track in forensic psychology from CUNY John Jay College. He nearly lost his medical license after one of his patients, Antoine Semius, revealed an improper doctor-patient sexual relationship. Antoine spoke of midnight rendezvous at the doctor's office, back alley sexual encounters, and a power dynamic that only served to belittle and mentally imprison Antoine.

After the news came out about Dr. Chardy's inappropriate behavior, two more patients came forward with similar stories. Dr. Chardy was temporarily suspended while an investigation took place. Mysteriously, Antoine Semius and another one of the accusers, Jacob Montenegro, disappeared off the face of the Earth, and shortly thereafter, the third accuser, Malcom Killebrew, withdrew his charge. He was later found dead in the Mexican resort town of Playa Del Carmen from an apparent suicide.

With no victims to question and no other evidence present, the medical review board had no choice but to allow Dr. Chardy to continue his practice without so much as a slap on the wrist. The bizarre circumstances of the investigation, however, left an uncomfortable microscope on Dr. Chardy, so he reluctantly left his practice six months later. After a year and a half of traveling the country running marathons, hiking national parks, and exploring the local gay nightlife of all the cities he visited, the call came in from Madame K that AWT had a position he might fit.

After an in-person interview at headquarters with Madame K, Ollie, and Li Xia, Dr. Chardy took just twenty-four hours to make his decision and accept the job offer presented to him at the interview. He officially started a week later.

Ollie and Li Xia have been watching a few people that might be good recruits for the next class at the academy. They meet outside of Madame K's office for a brief conversation before heading out to possibly approach one such person in Harlem.

Madame K emerges from her office. They greet each other and get down to business.

"You guys sure you don't want to take Edmond on this one?" Madame K asks. She's anxious to get him oriented to the process so a new class can begin at the Kill Academy, but she's been mostly hands-off when it comes to deciding when Dr. Chardy will be ready for the task. They can't bring in new recruits until he is fully involved in the process.

"Not this one," Ollie answers. "This recruit is a tricky one and we need to tread lightly at first or we'll scare him off."

Li Xia chimes in, "Dr. Chardy is close. In fact, we're planning a trip to visit another recruit in Chicago and he will come along and will be very hands-on."

"I trust you're doing the right thing. I just really want to move onto the next class ... and soon. But, again, I'll leave that to you."

"The real reason I wanted to speak to you before we leave is that we're going to be in Harlem all day," Ollie says. "And you know what's in Harlem?" Ollie is wide-eyed and suddenly excited.

"I'm guessing you are referring to Joe's barbeque?"

"Oh, you know I am. I'd like to bring back a spread for an early dinner for everyone. You okay with that?"

"Please do. Sounds wonderful. I'm sure everyone will be happy to share in it. Thank you."

"Perfect. We should be back no later than five."

"You people and your barbeque," Li Xia scoffs.

"Don't like, don't eat it," Ollie barks back, but playfully.

"I'll get dumplings from Han's."

"Come talk to me when you get back and give me the lowdown on the recruit." Madame K says.

"Of course," Ollie says. He looks to Li Xia. "We can take my car."

"Okay."

Madame K nods and returns to her office.

Ollie and Li Xia walk together to the parking deck and leave in Ollie's company SUV, driven by Ollie's personal and trusted driver.

On their way to Harlem, Ollie takes the opportunity in the privacy of the SUV to speak to Li Xia about his conversation with Josey.

"Guess who I talked to?" Ollie asks but doesn't slow down to get an answer. "It looks like it may be time to move on that little plan you came up with."

"I knew something was up," Li Xia says. "As soon as you came into my office this morning and said we needed to go check out a guy in Harlem. I knew it. So ... how's she doing?"

"She didn't say much, but like I figured, she sounded tired and basically over this shit. Live or die, she's ready to finish this."

"Good. I'm a little tired myself of this fake kissy-kissy bullshit we've been dishing out."

"You think there's any chance we make it out alive?"

"Honestly, I never felt we had much of a chance," Li Xia says with no hint of despair in her voice.

"Well, Jesus, Li." Ollie sighs loudly. "Remind me again why we should even go through with this?"

"Because we can't trust her anymore. And in this business, a business where trust is so hard to come by, once it leaves, it rarely returns. It will lead us all to the grave, eventually. So why not just take a chance now and hope for the best. The alternative seems worse to me."

"I know you're right. I just don't like it. And all of this over a girl from Baltimore."

"You know that's not true. The warning signs have been there for a while, like small tremors before the big quake. Whether Josey brought it out or not, it would have come regardless."

"Maybe."

"You think everyone is ready for this? Anybody gonna chicken out?"

"We're all locked in. One hundred percent."

"When will it begin?"

"If we're ready, I'll call her right now." Ollie pulls a phone from inside his suit coat.

"Go ahead then."

Ollie nods and swipes the screen of his phone to activate it. He dials the number and puts it to his ear.

The conversation with Josey went exactly as Ollie expected. To him, she seemed focused, calm, and just angry enough that it will serve her in this endeavor without it overwhelming her. As he spoke to her, he wondered if it might be the last time he ever would. He missed her face, her sharp attitude, her fire. He didn't want her to die but he knows there might not be much he can do about it. Such is life for a man entrenched in the world of contract assassination.

"Well?" Li Xia asks.

"She's going to send a message tomorrow, then she'll be on her way."

"Madame K is going to be pissed off like never before," Li Xia says as she slowly shakes her head.

"We're prepared for that."

"She may lash out. Could get ugly."

"Everything we do from here on out is a risk. We knew that going in. And we discussed this already."

"Just a friendly reminder. So, are we actually going to see this guy in Harlem or was that just an excuse to get us out of the building?"

"Yes, we're going. Can't deviate right now."

"Good. Let's focus on that then."

"Okay, Li. We're almost there anyway."

29

I'm on the road, again, but this time, instead of running away from a life I felt trapped in, I'm heading straight into the eye of the storm. I thought for sure I would be nervous and scared for what might happen, primarily my death, but I'm only slightly anxious. I happen to be ultra-focused, my mind on getting to the endgame.

I left the town of Burton without burning down the cabin. I decided it might draw unwanted attention to the fact I killed two guys there and buried them nearby. I drove their truck fifty miles away to a junk yard and gave the owner, Ramon, two thousand dollars to crush it into a scrap metal pancake and then forget he ever saw me.

I also wrote Farmer a note and dropped it in the mail. He was so incredibly kind to me; I didn't want to leave him hanging. If I had suddenly disappeared without saying goodbye, he might have contacted the police thinking an ex-boyfriend had abducted me, considering the story I had fed him early-on about why I was there. I kept the note short and sweet with no specifics. I hope the impact I leave is not ultimately a negative one.

I called Hakeem Miller, my old hacker buddy back in Baltimore, and had him help with a personal property distribution plan in case I don't make it out alive. I don't really have anything, save for some cash. The plan is, if I don't call Hakeem in two weeks, he is to ship a package I prepared to the Leer family. The box contains just two things. One is fifty-grand in cash, neatly stacked and wrapped. The second thing is a letter. With my newfound letter writing skills, I might be priming myself to begin work on my memoir. Josey Baldwin. Assassin. Ass-kicker. Author? Ha!

I have a few hours left in my drive from Baltimore to what might be my final destination. I've arranged through Ollie and Marty to be able to send a private message to Madame K, and I feel like now is the time for me to kick-off our little game.

I pull off the road when I spot a gas station and McDonald's combo. After scarfing down a burger, I get out my dummy phone, bring up text messaging, type in Madame K's private number, and begin the short message.

'Time's up. If you're wondering why, know this: It won't be about Rosemary. It won't be about Daniel. It won't be about Annie. Your death will be about YOU and ME. Start the countdown.'

My index finger hovers over the SEND button for an unnatural amount of time. I typed the message full of piss and vinegar, but now that it's time to take this whole thing to another level, I seem to be catatonic. My finger finally falls down to the screen and onto the SEND, lacking any sort of confidence.

There's no going back now. Madame K may not even react to the message in the way we expect. She could very well dismiss it out of hand and go on with business as usual. For now, that would be okay. The next phase of the plan, however, will likely force her hand, and that is where she and I will have a reckoning.

30

On the streets of New York City

On her way home from AWT and after gorging on the barbeque brought in by Ollie and Li Xia, Madame K sits in the backseat of her company town car with her head leaning back and her eyes closed. She ponders the last couple of months and how everything has seemed to normalize. There's a sense of relief yet she doesn't feel completely satisfied with how things have turned out. Josey is still at-large and that wildcard leaves a bad taste in her mouth. Even with all their resources, the loose end persists, and there is a part of her, despite the leadership saying otherwise, that believes some at the company are looking out for Josey, if not steering things away from her completely. If this is true, it means there is a lot of window-dressing going on AWT, and that, for Madame K, is unacceptable.

The implications of that kind of betrayal would be enormous, and she tries hard to expect better of her employees, but her trust for them is on a razor's edge. Some of their behavior, like the barbeque, seem almost obnoxiously peaceful. Then again, this may be the new normal. The morale within the company needed to change or else everything was bound to fall apart. Perhaps, she thinks, everyone wants desperately to move on and these behaviors are just minor overcompensations.

Madame K's personal driver, Lenny, interrupts her deep thoughts with a question. "You need me to stop off anywhere, ma'am?"

She opens her eyes, pulls her head forward, and lets out a deep sigh. "Not necessary. Just straight home. Thank you."

"Will do," Lenny answers.

A jingle sounds from inside Madame K's Gucci bag. She throws back the flap and removes the cell phone. There are only seven people with the number for this particular phone, her personal phone, so it's bound to be related to some matter of importance. She selects the text message on the lock screen and swipes right to open it.

Madame K reads the message once, quickly, then to verify the audacity of the words on the screen, she reads through it again with a more deliberate speed. She makes a mental note of the sender's number and how it's clearly fake. 1234567890.

She needs no time to process the message. The threat is clear and the sender is obvious. What pisses her off is how seemingly easy it was for Josey to get the number. Her first thoughts point to an inside assist.

"Ooooooohhh," she says as she slowly shakes her head. "Whomever helped you out, Miss Baldwin, had best not be revealed to me or their fate will match yours."

She closes the message and brings up a new one. She adds Li Xia, Dr. Chardy, and Ollie for a group message, then types the following:

'Mandatory leadership meeting in my office at 9 am sharp. URGENT. DO NOT BE LATE.'

She sends the message, closes out the phone, and returns it to her bag. She won't check for responses. They won't matter. When Madame K calls for a mandatory meeting, all other plans are canceled, period.

She spends the rest of her ride home contemplating the approach she will take regarding the message. By the time they pull up to her building, she has solidified her intentions and doesn't think about it again that evening.

31

I found a seedy motel a few miles away from my ultimate destination. I don't want to be bothered and there's no better place than a rural, roadside hooker palace for people who won't look you in the eye and will mind their own fucking business.

I got a room with two double beds. I need a place to lay out my stuff and still have a place to sleep. With what's on the horizon, I doubt I'll sleep much, if at all. I'd compare how I feel right now to someone on death row. In those last twenty-four, forty-eight, or seventy-two hours before the execution, I would guess the dead man walking can't fall asleep. If a person knows they are in their final hours, how could they spend it sleeping? The long nap is right around the corner. A few days from now, I might close my eyes and never wake up again. I'm both ready for it and terrified of it.

I laid my outfit and weaponry on the bed furthest from the door. The clothes are simple black cargo pants, black boots, a long sleeve black crewneck shirt, and a black zip-up hoodie. With the fire power, I'm keeping it super-simple. Three guns, 2 knives, and my new stun gun, nicknamed Thor. My brilliant plan is to underwhelm Madame K, so much so, she may let her guard down and make it easy for me. Well, it's a plan. I didn't say it was a good one.

I wonder what the chances are that she'll just pop in and say, *"You know what, Josey? You're right. I fucked up. I killed your parents and I deserve to die, so go ahead. Take me out. I'll happily take the bullet on this one."*

She does scare the shit out of me though, and Ollie has warned me on multiple occasions how fierce a killer she is. I've heard stories too. I probably have about the same chance as an icicle in hell to come out of this alive. The thing is, I just don't care about the odds. I care about righting a wrong. I care about getting vengeance for my parents, people who by all accounts were decent, hard-working folks that didn't deserve to die over some whistleblower bullshit.

I do see the hypocrisy in all this. How dare I, a paid assassin, get all bent out of shape over a grievance I've committed myself. Who could blame me though? We rarely get too worked up, too concerned about other people's problems so long as they don't touch us, but when they do, get out of the way motherfuckers, we about to burn the world down over this shit.

I haven't heard anything about the message I sent to Madame K, not that I expected to. Ollie and I agreed not to contact each other again while the plan is in motion, except for a final communication from him as to when they were going to execute their part of the plan, which would trigger me to send one final message to Madame K. He wants to minimize the chances of her finding out, which makes sense. The ultimate goal is for she and I to have a final showdown and we don't want anything to impede on that potential outcome. The only word I will get is when she's on her way here. Until then, I wait patiently.

To pass the time, I'll spend my days jogging, watching too many cute animal videos on the internet, dying my hair back to black, and drinking too much coffee. I might even take in a movie at a nearby small-town movie theater. I could use the distraction. My mind wants to wade through the muck and dread of the dark possibilities of my situation more than it wants to float through the hopeful ones. If I'm not careful, I might go insane with fear and doubt and just run away again. I know, somewhere inside, it's too late for that but I still worry I might.

Too bad Ollie isn't here, because let's be honest, being this close to my death, all I really want to do is get laid. Not that I couldn't just find some young buck in town, but I've never really been one for rando-sex. Jesus, I need to get out of this room and get some air. A good run will help me focus, burn some nervous energy.

It won't be long and I'll be sending a second message to Madame K, and if all goes to plan, it will be the fuse that lights her fire. Li Xia's idea to ensure Madame K comes to me better work. I think it will. We have no backup plan. If she doesn't bite, all hell may break loose.

32

Madame K's Office

Standing at her large office window looking outward, hands folded neatly on the small of her back, Madame K has said nothing for a full two minutes after Li Xia, Ollie, and Dr. Chardy had entered the room. They wait patiently. Li Xia and Ollie know exactly why they've been called. Dr. Chardy keeps looking over to the others for a clue to what's going on and how to handle the situation. They say nothing as they wait for their boss to begin.

"On my way home last night, I received a rather disturbing message. A death threat." Madame K pauses.

"From whom?" Li Xia asks.

"You know the answer to that. Our little orphan has decided to pick a fight."

"You can't possibly be worried?" Ollie asks.

"Just so I can keep up with this conversation, are we speaking about Josey Baldwin?" Dr. Chardy asks. He's been briefed but hasn't been intimately involved in any real action regarding her.

"Yes, Dr. Chardy, Josey is the culprit. And no, I'm certainly not worried about Josey Baldwin and her hollow threats. What does worry me is how she got my number."

Li Xia jumps back in, "I'll get Marty and Tisha on that right away. There has to be a way to track the source."

"I'm sure she's got hacker friends," Ollie says.

"Perhaps. Regardless. It's time to put our full efforts into bringing her in, dead or alive. I have no preference." Madame K decides not to reveal her suspicions about Josey getting inside help. She needs time to gauge the situation.

"Aren't we already doing that?" Li Xia asks.

Madame K turns around to face them.

"Apparently not. If we were already doing that, she wouldn't be out there starting shit. If I don't get some results in the next few days, I'll send *you*," she points first at Li Xia, then to Ollie, "... both out there to get her personally."

"Okay," Ollie says.

Li Xia says nothing and remains as stoic as always.

Madame K locks eyes with Ollie. "And let me assure you, if I find out anyone is helping her, it's game over."

Ollie gave her a smirk, that without actually saying anything, begged the question, 'Really?'

"Can I say something here?" asks Dr. Chardy.

"What?" Madame K barks.

Dr. Chardy's eyes go a little wide at the snap. "I'd love to be able to chime in and help but I don't exactly understand the full scope of what's going on? Could someone give me a little background, otherwise, I don't really see why you called me in here."

"When I call a meeting of the leadership core, this is who attends," Madame says but pauses for a moment to consider his point, "but in this case, I think you might be correct. Get out."

"Okay," Dr. Chardy concedes, both accepting and a little put-out by the abrupt and cold nature of the command. He glances over to Li Xia for confirmation and she gives him a quick nod. He leaves without saying another word.

"Now," Madame K continues, "I want every available asset on finding her. No new contracts until this is done. Where is Amatto?"

"He's in the field on the Burke job," Ollie says.

"How soon until he's done?"

"A matter of days, I would guess."

"Good. He joins the fray immediately upon finishing his work.

"He's not going to like that. He needs his reset time."

"I don't give a shit what *he* needs."

Ollie puts his hands up. "We'll get it done then. Enough is enough. Let's finish this."

"Good," Madame K says, nodding her head. "Good. I want regular updates."

"Well, we have a lot of work to do, so, is that it then?" Li Xia asks.

"Go on then," Madame K responds.

Ollie and Li Xia leave the room.

Madame K turns back around and stares out of the window, losing track of time. A few minutes pass. She manages not to linger too long on the worst parts of what might lie ahead. She's always been pragmatic, decisive, emotionless, crass even, when it came to job related issues, but as she takes in her view of the city, a bit of reluctance finds a way into her mind, enough to make her doubt her own choices and thought processes.

She closes her eyes and covers her face with her hands, rubbing her forehead with her fingertips. She then lowers her arms and rotates her neck in a full circle to release the tension.

Madame K whispers, despite the fact no one could hear her unless they were in the room, "One bad decision twenty some years ago, and this is what I get? Well, this little girl is not going to be the end of me. I've been through too much to let one little over-zealous bitch bring me down. Not going to happen. And I'll tear this whole fucking place apart if necessary."

33

I'm out for a morning jog, trying hard to keep my sanity. It's damn cold and getting to a point where I will no longer be able to avoid wearing a coat when I go out, or at least put on enough layers to have the same effect.

I received a message from Ollie last night. He said the time had come for me to send one final message to Madame K, in the seven o'clock hour, and that as of tomorrow morning, the plan would be in full-motion and nonretractable. There would be no further communication until after the dust has settled. The finality of his statements left me uneasy, and the only thing I could do to keep from going mad was to run. So here I am, doing just that on the backroads of rural America.

I dreamt of Tom and Dina last night. It was weird. The two of them kept morphing into each other like they were the same person. I suppose, in some way, they both served a similar purpose in my life, you know, with all that life wisdom and psycho-babble. I don't recall the fine details of the dream, just the feelings it left me with. Saddened. Vexed. And yet, a little hopeful.

On my way back to the tiny town where my motel is, I stop at the lone gas station, grab some food, including a box of donuts, a bag of cheese puffs, a few chocolate bars, and a 2-liter of diet soda. Not exactly my finest moment in the low-carb world I try to reside in, but part of me said fuck it. It won't be my last meal, although, it's starting to feel that way. I can imagine that in the next forty-eight hours I will inhale an unnatural amount of pizza, French fries, and candy. I should probably be careful though. If I get into a fight to the death, the last thing I need is to feel dumpy from too much bread. I just really need this shit to be over with.

After watching back-to-back rom-coms and falling asleep to some animal show on Nat-Geo, I awake to the sound of my phone alarm telling me the time had come to send the last message. Once I do this, I'll have nothing left to do but wait until she shows up, assuming she does. What happens then is anyone's guess. I will let my instincts guide me through to whatever end may arise. That's all I can do.

I type the message and press send with no hesitation. I sure hope everything is in place on Li Xia and Ollie's end. Without their part in all this, I will have been wasting my damn time. I've put my full trust in them. I have considered the possibility this whole thing is one big charade and a massive backstab. I doubt they'd do that to me, but let's be real, they're either backstabbing me or doing so to Madame K, so they are, in fact, capable of it. The question is whether their loyalty lies with me or with her. As anyone would, they are really looking out for what they believe is best for themselves, and that's okay. In their shoes, I'd do the same. I just hope their goals align with my own.

I can imagine when Madame K reads my message this time, she might blow a gasket. Anyone nearby had better hope she doesn't have a weapon on her at the time.

I thought I might go out and grab dinner, but I'm so mentally exhausted, I think I'll just get a pizza delivered and stay up all night binge-watching absolutely anything not related to killing and murderous revenge. With any luck, I'll fall asleep with no effort. A girl can hope.

34

Madame K's high-rise apartment in the Greenwich Village area of Manhattan

Feeling it necessary to compensate for her overindulgence in the barbeque from the other night and a heavy bread and pasta-laden dinner tonight, Madame K changes to an all-black yoga outfit and is on the treadmill. At 7:14 p.m., her evening wind-down glass of chardonnay would have to wait until she felt sufficiently rid of the excess calories. In this case, she believes a forty-five-minute run will do the trick.

She had her treadmill placed in front of a large window that overlooked the Hudson. Eleven stories up, she has a spectacular view of the water and the cityscape across from it. The sunsets alone raise the value of her property by a considerable amount, and that is on top of the existing New York real estate swell. At this hour though, just past dusk, the view is illuminated with the glow and sparkle of a city still running at full speed. Having spent so much of her early adult life living in the shadows of the night, she now prefers the daylight. The beauty, however, of the New York City evening skyline is not lost on her.

After taking in the splendor for a moment, she places her cellphone on the console in front of her, the same place someone might place a tablet or a book, and she hits the start button.

At first, she regrets the idea of running so soon after a big meal but she presses on despite this, and fifteen minutes in, hits her stride, light on her feet and sweating just enough to feel like she's working.

Interrupting the rhythmic beat of her feet hitting the rubber, her phone jingles to life. She picks it up and swipes the screen with a moist finger.

The message reads:

'What will you do when you can't stand behind other people? Once you realize how alone you are, meet me at the place it all began and we'll finish this.'

She stops the treadmill and places the phone back down on the console. She uses the towel hanging from the support bar and aggressively wipes her hands and face before returning the towel to the bar.

Angry sparks ignite in her eyes. She wants to smash something. She thinks about tossing the phone across the room or smashing a lamp, but decides instead to finish her workout. Wouldn't be the first time she ran through a bout of frustration.

She starts the treadmill back up, increasing the speed, hoping to release the tension.

Her formerly light steps are now pounding and heavy. The sweat builds, her breathing quickens, but somehow, the anger does not subside.

After an unsatisfying four minutes, Madame K stops the treadmill, skipping her usual five-minute cooldown walk by just hopping straight off, grabbing her phone and the sweaty towel before heading down the hall to shower.

The master bathroom is almost entirely white and gray Carrera marble shipped directly from Italy. The bathroom remodel was the first project she had completed after moving in.

She places her phone near the sink and strips off her exercise outfit, placing it and the exercise towel in the hamper.

With the shower on full-hot, the bathroom steams up in

less than two minutes. Upon entering the tiled shower, she leans into the falling water to let it caress her neck and flow freely down her back. She closes her eyes. Her breathing calms. Her thoughts focus. What she believes is the truest path going forward begins to unfold in her mind.

Flashes of the faces of her top employees at AWT appear. Nazir, Tisha, Marty, Greg, Li Xia, Ollie. Marty lingers a bit longer than the rest but Ollie's face is the one that seems distorted. Ugly. His relationship with Dina and Josey suggests to Madame K a weakness, a struggle to stay loyal.

She wants to dismiss this idea. It almost seems too easy, too obvious. Plus, if she trusted anyone explicitly, it would be Ollie. She personally trained him as an assassin and has groomed him to be her successor for years. She would acknowledge they've had many differences in opinion over the years, especially recently, but that never got in the way of their relationship.

In this moment, Madame K finally lets an idea sink in, an idea she has somehow understood all along but never wanted to concede because doing so would mean admitting she made a colossal mistake. Despite already admitting what she did with Josey over twenty years ago, she has always blamed Josey for the recent escalation of the internal hostility at AWT. Deep in her mind and soul, with the hot water flowing over her like a cleanse of truth, she finally accepts her own responsibility. She's never thought of herself as living without flaws or incapable of mistakes, but she's always done a remarkable job of avoiding or at least minimizing them. A person doesn't last long in the assassin game without doing so. A tinge of vulnerability slips in, a sensation she rarely experiences.

Josey Baldwin must die, she decides. *The rift created by her presence is too big to overcome. With any luck, AWT will return to its previous condition once she's out of the picture.*

It pisses her off that Josey hasn't been located yet, and it's creating a great deal of suspicion about each of her staff members. The variable in their world, however, is Josey

Baldwin. Solve for the variable and the answer to the equation is clear.

She didn't want it come to this. There's a slight hesitancy for her in the idea of having Josey killed, a notion she chuckles at. They're all in the business of killing people, violently, wantonly, yet killing this one person gives her pause for reasons she can't decipher. She thinks about how nice it would be if she could speak to Dina about it. Certainly, she would've had some insight into why Josey should matter so much in the grand scheme of things. The fact she cannot speak to her trusted advisor reignites her anger.

She finishes her shower, dries off, wraps the towel around her head, puts on the white robe hanging on the back of the bathroom door, and walks with her phone in hand out to the kitchen. She brings up a group text message and alerts her leadership core, minus Dr. Chardy, that once again, there will be a mandatory meeting in her office at nine am sharp.

Still fuming from Josey's audacity, she walks over to the sink, places the phone into the drain, and with her index finger, slides the phone all the way in. After turning the hot water to full, she hits the wall switch for the garage disposal. The cracking and scrapping are like nails on a chalkboard, the motor stuttering a few times like it's ready to quit, but she lets it go. After ten seconds, she stops it, lets out a deep sigh, and feels a bit better.

"No more goddamn messages from Josey Baldwin."

She steps to the fridge to retrieve a chilled bottle of wine that she'll finish quickly.

35

From the personal journal of Dina Whiteside
Two days before the first time she met Josey

It's been thirteen months since our most recent Kill Team "disbanded", with Amatto, now elevated to solo assassin, being the only one left from that class. We've had a few sessions, as required by company policy, to discuss what happened, now over a year ago, but he remains less than forthcoming. I could have easily kept Amatto from being promoted because of his lack of cooperation. I mean, I asked all the questions and probed in all the usual ways, and he has always answered, but he's too smart for his own good. He just gives me the straight-forward, most clinical answer he can think of that will keep his personal career development moving and his finger on the trigger. My ego is what allowed me to let him pass. I just figured at some point I would break through and get him to trust me. I'm still working on it.

This leads me to our current endeavor. We are now closing in on a new group of recruits to bring in for evaluation. We have the usual course of social outcasts, business and government deviants, and criminal line-riders.

There's one we're eyeing who is of particular interest and

curiosity. The young woman from Baltimore has a real vigilante thing going. She seems to be wandering through life, keeping an eye out for creepy and nefarious males in her area that look to do women harm. When she spots one such creep, she intervenes, often beating the living crap out of them to teach them a lesson. Blackmail usually follows. Between that and the occasional small-time heist, she survives.

As far as we can tell though, she has never intentionally taken a life, not aside from self-defense. In fact, she's appears completely averse to killing. She has no interest in firearms, carrying only knives and a stun gun. Granted, killing someone comes with great and substantial risk, so perhaps she is just playing the odds. She wants to continue living her life and being free, and if she were to decide to kill some of these thugs she deals with on a regular basis, she would significantly increase her chances of getting caught by the authorities, or at the very least, she'd draw too much attention in the dark underworld she lives in to stay safe for very long.

She's also fiercely independent and appears to have a chip on her shoulder that's less chip and more bowling ball, but her penchant for helping the helpless could be an angle we can use to get her onboard with AWT. My guess is that she'll flat-out reject us. After sharing my concerns with Madame K, Ollie, and Li Xia about her, we were instructed specifically to pursue the woman anyway. And our best efforts were expected. I took that as a directive. I have wondered why Madame K took this unusual stance, as she has never suggested anything like this with other recruits, from this class or past ones. Perhaps she sees a little of herself in this Josey Baldwin? I'll certainly monitor this development. Anything out of the norm is worth keeping tabs on.

Ollie and I are planning our initial meeting with Josey. There's a coffee shop she frequently visits not far from the houseboat she currently occupies, so our plan is to keep showing up in her peripherals, forcing her to get just curious enough to try and follow us. The technique almost always works, especially if I am the visible one. I think my appearance and the fact that I'm a woman make me less intimidating, and thusly, less likely to be threatening or from some government agency trying to trap the person.

Either way, we're getting close. From a purely professional perspective, this potential class of recruits has me, dare I say, almost excited. They have such a varied mix of backgrounds and experiences that I relish the opportunity to evaluate them as a psychologist. While most people in this business have many similarities, I have discovered they are as different as fingerprints in many more ways. I can't wait to have them in the building.

36

Just before 9 a.m. at AWT

The headquarters of AWT, short for Advanced Weapons Tech, is essentially a front company for Madame K's business of contract assassination. AWT's other business, however, is a legit one, in that they design, manufacture, and sell exactly what their name implies. The contract assassination business happens to benefit from this front. They can create unique and untraceable weapons for use in fulfilling their contracts, a massive benefit in their trade.

These two businesses exist in the same space but they rarely overlap. The building in New York City, a brash attempt to hide in plain sight, is split into three sections.

The top floor is the executive level and is occupied by Madame K and her secretary Jessica. There are three conference rooms and two bathrooms that are rarely used, a few spaces used just for storage, a private exercise room for Madame K's use only, and a kitchen and dining space mostly used by Jessica.

All the floors from the ground floor to just beneath the executive level are occupied by the inner workings of the legitimate side of AWT. The company employs nearly five hundred people that include all the usual departments of a company that size. They have their own in-house marketing, sales, and accounting teams to keep third parties from finding out the truth. There are only five people in this part of AWT that ever have contact with Madame K: The vice president, who has no knowledge of the contract assassination business, and six others who have been planted in the engineering, accounting, and manufacturing areas to shade the minor connections to the assassination side.

The basement levels of the building are where the heart of the Kill Academy and the contract assassination business reside. And there's never any danger of the wrong people wandering where they don't belong. All doors, and even the elevators, are activated by key fobs that each employee must have on them at all times. Each fob is encoded with information for each person and their specific access. Every single door in the building, right down to the bathrooms, has this system installed.

The basement levels, most often referred to, secretly, as the Kill Academy, is where the offices of Ollie, the Dean, Greg, Nazir, and now Dr. Chardy are located. There are bunk rooms, a cafeteria, bathrooms, an exercise room, medical facilities, and training spaces.

On the average day, most of the building is bustling like any office building does, and this day is no exception. Madame K arrives at around eight-thirty each weekday morning via her personal driver. He drops her off at a special elevator in the parking deck that only she is allowed to use. Once she reaches the top floor, she stops for a moment to chat with Jessica about her daily schedule.

"Good morning, ma'am. How are you today?" Jessica is professional without fail, a proper executive assistant in dress, demeanor, and loyalty. Now in her early sixties, she's been with Madame K since almost the beginning, and has seen the best and the worst of her boss and what the works entails. She answers to no one but Madame K.

"In all honesty, I didn't sleep well. I have a meeting with leadership again for nine this morning. Please clear my schedule until one. I have some phone calls I need to make after the meeting."

"Will do. Is there anything I can get you? Your usual tea or something stronger, perhaps?"

"Tea is fine. I don't have much of an appetite. Maybe throw together a plate of jack cheese, a few green grapes, and ... a few thin slices of tomato. Just in case I discover I can stomach something."

"I'll have it to you shortly, ma'am."

"Thank you. As they arrive this morning, let them right in to my office."

Jessica stands, ready to head to the kitchen. "Of course. I'll be just a moment." She hustles off to prep her boss' breakfast and tea.

Madame K enters her office, uses the restroom, then settles into her desk chair, mentally going over what she will say to the leadership core when they arrive.

With her last text message, Josey Baldwin threw down a gauntlet, one created in their mutual history of blood and death. Despite the acknowledgement of her own responsibility in the current upheaval, Madame K still holds a strong instinct for self-preservation, one she can't ignore. Shrouding all of this is her ego. In the grand scheme of both their lives, Madame K is certain that her own life means more than that Josey's, and this somehow alleviates any remorse or obligated sense of fairness that might be expected from someone having admitted fault. She can see only one way forward and the time had come to escalate.

Jessica enters the office with a tray in hand. She places it on a small side table to her left, then grabs the tea and the Wall Street Journal from it. She walks over and hands the paper directly to Madame K and places the tea to the left edge of the desk.

"Would you like the food now or should I place in the fridge?" asks Jessica.

Madame K unfolds the newspaper and browses the front page. "Go ahead and put it away. I might nibble later if my appetite returns." A hint of the lemon from her tea wafts over, enticing her to take a sip before continuing to read.

Jessica returns to the table, takes the plastic wrapped plate and puts in on the top shelf of the mini refrigerator near the bathroom door. The only other items in the refrigerator are two glass bottles of sparkling water and four plastic bottles of regular water.

From back at the head of the desk, Jessica asks, "Do you need anything else, ma'am?"

Madame K lowers the paper. "Actually, yes. There was a little ... mishap with my personal phone last night. I need Tisha or Marty to get me another one, same protocols as before."

"I'll call down there immediately. Anything else?"

"That's it for now. Thank you."

"Of course." Jessica leaves the room. The door shuts behind her.

Madame K reads her paper, polishes off her tea, and is starting to feel like she might be able to eat something when it dawns her that it might be close to nine o'clock. She looks down to her wristwatch. In fact, it's two minutes after nine. She taps the face of her watch and assumes it must be broken or fast. She flips open her laptop. The time in the lower righthand corner reads 9:03 AM. She's almost befuddled.

"Somebody better be dead," she says, rising from her chair. She walks around her desk to leave and when she reaches the door, throws it open in disgust.

The sudden commotion startles Jessica. She immediately stands but says nothing.

"Call down to Ollie and ask him why the hell he's not up here?"

"Yes, ma'am." She sits back down, picks up the receiver of her office phone, and dials Ollie's extension. She waits patiently for a response. None comes. She looks to Madame K and shakes her head.

Madame K's eyes grow wide. "Try Li Xia."

"Yes, ma'am." She ends the call and dials a new extension. Jessica understands the unusual nature of what is happening. She can feel her stomach tensing up. There is no answer on the other end. She shakes her head again.

"God damn it!" Madame K slams her hand down on the edge of Jessica's desk. "I need a phone. What did the techies say about me getting a new one?"

"I'm sorry, ma'am, they haven't arrived for work yet. There's been no answer to my queries. Direct message or by phone."

An idea starts to creep into Madame K's mind, an idea centered around betrayal. She quickly dismisses the notion, instead choosing to believe there must be some other explanation.

She storms off to the elevator that everyone else uses instead of her private one, and once inside, presses the button that will take her to the basement.

When the doors open, she marches to Ollie's office. She throws open his door to find it empty. Without hesitation, she does the same to Li Xia's office with the same result. She turns around, stops to take in her surroundings, and finds an eerie silence, not that this area is ever lively with activity, but it struck her as odd.

Dr. Chardy emerges from his office and to find Madame K standing oddly in the hallway.

"Good morning," he says.

"Have you seen or heard from Ollie or Li Xia?" She walks over to him.

"Not since yesterday. Why?"

"We were supposed to have a meeting at nine and they haven't showed."

"That's odd."

"Beyond odd. Fuck." Madame K rubs her left temple. She turns and walks away, heading toward The Bridge. She presses open the door to find a dark room, only the LED lights of computers, networking gear, and other equipment illuminating the space. Tisha and Marty are both absent.

She leaves the doorway and checks around for Nazir, Greg, and Vick. They are nowhere to be found either. Slightly out of breath, she closes her eyes for a moment and attempts to assess the situation. She smiles and nods her head, impressed by the audacity of their actions.

Back in the hallway, she speaks aloud but to no one in particular. "This is clearly some orchestrated plan to unnerve me, maybe undermine me. I can see now that all of you have made a choice to back Miss Baldwin, and for that, you have claimed your end."

She whips around to find Dr. Chardy right behind her.

"Is something wrong?" he asks.

"It would appear a mutiny is underway. I assume you had no knowledge of this?"

"Mutiny? Jesus. No. What the hell is going on?"

"My past is catching up to me. You might as well go home. I'll call you when it's safe to return. I don't know what they have planned and you could be in danger."

"Are you sure I can't help with something, anything?"

"No. Just leave. Now!"

Madame K uses her private elevator this time, and after getting off, she passes Jessica's desk, and without missing a stride says, "clear my entire schedule for the next week."

"Yes, ma'am."

Madame K enters her office and sits down behind her desk. She pulls a disposable phone from a drawer and turns it on. She stops for a moment and wonders who she can call at time like this considering her entire staff seems to have abandoned her. She thinks, *I have friends outside of AWT, although the word friend may be a stretch. Acquaintances, contacts, former lovers. I've clearly isolated myself too much.*

She suddenly remembers Josey's last message about being alone. For the first time, she fully understands how deep the betrayal runs. By her best estimate, their big meeting after

Dina's death is when the entire charade officially began. From out of the blue, everyone seemed to be cooperative and moving on. The environment around the office had reverted to a state that existed prior to Josey Baldwin. Madame K had her doubts at that time as to how genuine the turn-around was, but she pushed on, choosing to believe in the people she hired and surrounded herself with. Now, the mistakes in her judgement were adding up, and she could feel the weight of her choices bearing down in a way she had never experienced.

Looking down to her hands, there was a slight tremble. For the first time in as long as she could remember, she felt vulnerable. It made no sense to her. She had put down fierce groups of thugs, Iranian bodyguards, high-profile government officials, yet little Josey Baldwin, a newcomer in their business, set her nerves ablaze. She simply could not reconcile the effect.

Out of the corner of her eye, she notices a message has popped up on her laptop. She puts the phone down and clicks the icon on her computer screen to open the instant message.

From: The Reckoning
To: Madame K
Message: What are you waiting for? Come Armed. Come Alone.

Madame K slams her laptop closed, yanks it off the desk, breaking it free from the networking and power cords, and tosses it overhead with both hands across the room toward the entry door. It smashes hard into the wall and lands on the floor, the CD tray ejected and bent, but the rest relatively unharmed. Using both hands, she thrashes and scatters everything from her desk, spilling it all onto the floor.

She grabs the gun hidden under her desk, stand ups, and fires the entire clip into the backs of the chairs in front of her desk. The walls of her office are nearly soundproof, so Jessica, who is a just a few feet from the door hears a slight rustling noise but doesn't think much of it.

"Oooooohhh ... she has no fuckin' idea who she's dealing with. You come in here, you dissect my people and tear my company apart. But there's no going back now, is there? As far as I'm concerned, every damn one of you is dead."

Breathing heavy and fed up, she finds the disposable cell phone on the floor and leaves. It would be hard for anyone to understand what happened to the office, now in shambles.

"Ma'am, I've been trying to get in contact with everyone by any means I can, and I'm getting no response. Is everything okay?" Jessica is beginning to sound panicked. She fully understands what is happening. She hears more than people realize, but she never discusses the business in this manner with her boss.

"Have the jet and the crew ready for a flight to Pennsylvania. I'll be ready to leave at noon. I need to go home to pack for the trip, so call my driver to the deck."

"Of course. Anything else, ma'am?"

"From my personal account number eight, please transfer five million dollars to your own account. Write it up as a severance from AWT."

"Ma'am, I don't understand."

"Yes you do. After you do those other things, immediately begin shutdown protocol. Unfortunately, our time here is over. And thank you, Jessica, you've been a near perfect assistant to me. My life has been made easier having you here. So, again, thank you."

Stunned, Jessica cannot find the words to respond.

"If we're lucky, maybe someday we can sit and enjoy a cocktail on some beach and reminisce about our time together," Madame K says with all due sincerity, the first words she has ever spoken to Jessica that were purely as a friend and not her boss.

Jessica is close to breaking down but summons the courage to keep her emotions together. She smiles and nods.

"And thank you for allowing me to serve you for all these years, and for your generosity. I will see your final instructions done, then be on my way, if that's okay?"

"Yes. Don't linger around here. I have no idea what the others are planning, so better to stay clear of it. Go on a trip. If I make it out alive, I'll be in touch. Goodbye, Jessica."

"Goodbye, ma'am."

"From now on, you can call me Madeline."

37

Rural Pennsylvania

Madame K can remember every kill and every location in which she performed one. That is both a consequence of her phenomenal memory and an occupational hazard. When preparing for any kill mission, the Point scouts the surroundings, studies maps and blueprints, and after a time, they know them as much as they know their own homes and offices. The Point must study the people too - their habits, their movements, how many times a day they piss, eat, have sex. By doing all this, the faces of these people and the places they occupy become more or less permanently etched in the minds of the assassin. As Madame K arrives to the now dilapidated house near Hampton Township, the place she murdered Daniel and Anzu Jones and kidnapped their daughter Kiki, she is no exception to the high-level retention that comes with being an assassin.

Before hitting the driveway and pulling in, Madame K first stopped a mile away, and using a high-powered scope, surveyed the area in all directions leading up to the property. She didn't believe there would be any sort of ambush but she wanted to be certain. This situation, however, was about vengeance. Josey, like any trained assassin that found themselves under these circumstances, would need to meet their foe eye-to-eye, and using their skill, end the game in a fair fight.

When she does finally decide to arrive at around four in the afternoon, Madame K pulls the black sedan into the driveway and stops after twenty feet, just to assess the property. From her visual memory, everything is different, yet still the same. The house is still standing, although, it looks like it hasn't been occupied for twenty years. Many of the windows are broken, the roof is in serious disrepair, and there's no front door. She can imagine all the insects, birds, and animals that have made it home over the years. She cringes at the idea of how it must smell.

Off to her left, there is a large walnut tree that catches her attention, easily over a hundred years old and too tall to see much of the top. What's important is the envelope pinned to it with a serrated black hunting knife, about five feet up from the ground. In black ink and large capital letters, M.K., is written on it.

"I guess we're pen pals now," Madame K says as she exits the vehicle. She's constantly looking in all directions for anyone that might be trying to catch her off-guard. She's here to confront Josey, but she hasn't forgotten that all the others at AWT have abandoned her and may be looking for blood too. If that happened here, she's under no illusion that she'd be outgunned, so she tries not to worry about that.

The air has a late-fall chill to it and the skies have turned gray, releasing a light drizzle that will only serve to make it feel colder. Adrenaline and her all-black tactical outfit will help keep the weather from becoming an issue. Much like Josey, she's chosen to keep her artillery simple. A few guns, a few blades, and a few surprises, in case things get weird or go horribly wrong.

She plucks the knife from the tree. After securing the envelope with her left hand, she returns the blade to the exact place she found it. "Such cheap knives these people buy. If it's not Japanese steel, it might as well have come from a local bait and tackle store. Jesus. Have some respect for the trade."

For a little cover, she walks over to a spot behind her car and pulls the letter out, then drops the envelope. She unfolds the paper and reads through it aloud.

"There is no one here but you and me. We're both here for the same reason, you to kill me and me to kill you. Before we get to the business of finally ending this, let's at least have an honest conversation. On my honor as an assassin, no shots will be fired by me until after we've spoken. No tricks. So, come on in."

There's been enough backstabbing at AWT in recent months to give Madame K pause to the invitation. *Josey may have offered her word, but Ollie, the Dean, and the others have not,* she thinks. *Well, I didn't implode my own company, sit on a plane for ninety minutes, and get all dressed up to turn back now.*

Madame K pops the strap from the weapon at her waist and cautiously steps toward the house, still guarded and glancing around for traps. She hits the doorway and pauses for a moment to look around before stepping through. Standing in the corner to her left is Josey. There is enough light coming through the holes in the roof and the windows to see. They are both wearing similar outfits, all black, tactical, light on the weaponry. Whatever ends up happening, it won't last long.

If Josey were taller, it would be like she was looking at a mirror image of herself from twenty or more years ago. The irony is not lost on her. She remembers the first time they ever laid eyes on each other. Thirty feet from where they now stand, Josey was at the bathroom sink and spotted Madame K in the mirror just moments after the woman had killed her parents. *Fitting,* she thinks. *I'm glad you brought us here. You can die in exactly the same place you should have back then.*

38

I've never seen Madame K like this, geared up and ready to kill. Even at her age, seeing her in this form scares the shit out of me. I dismiss the fear. I can't be standing here thinking she's going to win. I have to rise up and believe I'm in the right and that will propel me to victory. If I let any doubt slip in, I'm dead, period.

We stare at each other for an uncomfortable thirty seconds.

Finally, she speaks, "Looks like you've managed to build a little coalition against me. Well done. Not an easy task."

"You did that yourself by being a heartless bitch."

"Now, now. There's no need for that."

"Don't speak to me like I'm a child or your em-ploy-ee. I don't answer to you, not anymore."

"I was paying you a compliment. You've done something I wouldn't have thought possible, but here we are." Madame K takes one step to her left, out of the light of the doorway and into a spot more shadowed. "So, what are you so desperate to talk about?"

"Do you feel any remorse for killing my parents?"

"Hmmm. How many people have you killed, Miss

Baldwin, as an official assassin?"

"You can call me Kiki. I mean, that's who I was when you snatched me away from here. And I have no idea how many people I've killed."

"Yes, you do. I remember every single one of mine, their faces, their names. We, in this rarified line of work, always remember them. They burn themselves into our souls, if we have souls. So, don't lie to me. We're way past mind games. How many?"

"You're right," I relent. "I do know but I don't see how it matters at this moment."

"Do *you* feel remorse for killing any of them? Some surely had families, children that cared about them."

"It's different."

"Because it's personal to you?"

"Well, yeah."

"How short-sighted. Shame. In all candor and fairness, your parents were a contract, and for that I feel nothing. You should have been killed too. And for that I would have felt nothing. What I did with you instead, I can stand here and admit a little regret, if that's what you want to hear."

I expected nothing less from Madame K. She's not the kind of person who regrets the things she does. She's calculating, manipulative, and exacting. I kind of knew how she'd answer, I just wanted to hear her actually say the words. Leaves me with no doubt about ending her.

"I don't know what I want to hear. I feel wronged and I want you to pay. For me, it's really as simple as that. And if anyone I've ever killed feels the same about me, I wouldn't blame them. I would fight like hell to survive if they wanted to kill me, but I would understand."

"And there it is. Our instinct to survive. It can't be ignored. You have a wisdom beyond your years. I'm actually impressed. You could've gone far in this business, maybe even replaced me one day."

"If you think buttering me up is going to change my mind about wanting to kill you, you're sorely mistaken."

"You wanted an honest discussion. That's what I'm giving you."

"My life had a trajectory that was completely uprooted, not just because you killed my parents, but because you stole me away from here, placed me with Rosemary, of all fucking people, and set my life down a path. To what? Being you? I don't want to be you. I'm better than you." I'm trying to aggravate her. If she's becoming so, she is not showing it, but we're both starting to fidget.

"As it turns out, that is truer than you may realize. I plucked you from here because I once had an idea of raising and training assassins from a young age. You were to be my first attempt. Let me tell you, none of my colleagues at the time thought it was a good idea, but when I saw you standing in the bathroom all those years ago, the notion would not leave me alone. That idea saved your life."

"So, you did me a favor? Is that how you see it? Jesus, you're fucked up." I rub my forehead. The revelation that she was going to train me at that age to be an assassin terrifies me. I see the dark world of assassins as being a place for adults. Involving kids in any way is just wrong to me.

"Aren't we all? I don't think a person could be in this business and not be a little ... fucked up, as you say."

"I assume that ending up at AWT wasn't an accident. How come you didn't train me when I was younger?"

"The short answer is that time got away from me. After leaving you in Rosemary's care, I truly thought I would be back within the year to bring you under my roof and begin the process. The timing just never seemed right and after a while," Madame K shrugs her shoulders, "I started to have doubts I could do it, so I lost interest."

"That's about as cruel as it gets."

"It was. But let me assure you, I had nothing to do with your recruitment as an adult. That was an unhappy accident, as it turns out. But it's been a long day, so, unless you have any other brilliant insights you'd like to share, I say we get on with it."

"Best idea you've had today."

I don't feel ready for what is about to happen, but nonetheless, it's here.

I try to take one second to think about how I should proceed, but the blade coming at my chest instantly puts me on the defense.

I twist to my left just in time to avoid taking that knife to my heart. Fuck, her aim is amazing. The knife is now lodged three inches deep into the wall behind me.

I grab the gun from the holster on my back right hip and sprint through the archway into what used to be my family's dining room. As I run, I fire off three shots toward where I think Madame K might be. I immediately go through a second archway into the kitchen and duck behind a wall to the right, next to the fridge. There's garbage around, no real furniture, and thin walls, so there's no decent cover in here. I'm doubting my choice to duel in this house. I just couldn't resist the historical angle.

I peek around the corner. I see Madame K standing where I was originally in the living room. I imagine she's recovered her knife.

My heart is pumping out of my chest, the adrenaline high, but I am focused and calm, at least as much as I can be. I'm trying to think of something clever to say but nothing good comes to mind. We're staring at each other now.

Madame K breaks the silence, "Is this really necessary?" Her arm goes up and she fires five quick shots.

I pull my head back just in time. The brittle plaster around the archway explodes from two of the bullets. Three manage to get through to the kitchen, leaving holes in one of the upper cabinets to my right. I return three blind shots but guarantee they miss the mark. I open the fridge and get behind the door as a shield.

"No, it's not necessary at all. You could just throw down your weapons and let me have this."

She chuckles. "Not gonna happen, but I do understand how you feel. I too have a past, ya know. You're not special.

A person doesn't get into this industry without bringing a truckload of baggage."

"We're way past this making sense. Just admit it, there's no way forward in which we both live and just part ways."

"You set my entire world on fire," Madame K says, clearly bitter, "and now you think you should just be able to walk away?"

"That's a bit dramatic."

"You clearly have no idea what you've done."

"What *I've* done? This entire situation revolves around what *you* did. Everything that's happened since then has been in response to *your* actions. If you're not able to accept your true place in this, I don't see much point dancing around the topic."

I pop my arm around the corner and unleash a myriad bullets, emptying my clip. I toss the gun across the room and pull the gun from my left thigh.

"You're wasting ammo," Madame K says right before she does the same thing. Ten shots pierce the wall, some making it through to the fridge door, but none all the way to me.

"You're one to talk." I'm growing tired of the chitchat. I'm sure she is too. I wonder how likely I could get to her if I just charge. I think I could take her in hand-to-hand combat. There's no way at her age she could defeat me. I hope. Fuck it. I'm going.

I run out from behind the wall, letting loose a blaze of gunfire in a random pattern in the direction of Madame K. I've caught her off-guard.

She slinks back as I reach her, attempting to bring her gun down but it's too late. Simultaneously, we each get our free hand around the wrist of the other's weapon arm. Her grip is powerful. I may have made a mistake. Her squeeze forces me to drop my gun.

I'm pushing against her arm as hard as I can but her gun is still managing to creep close to my head. I need my dominate leg for leverage, so I use my left one to kick her in the shin. The pain forces her to release her grip. Instinctually, I do the same. I grab her gun by the barrel and use my free hand to unsheathe a knife from my belt, plunging it deep into her side, just above the kidney.

She buckles but keeps hold of her gun. She fires the final few bullets from the clip, all going into the ceiling.

I let go of her gun and my knife. She strikes me across the face with the gun, then drops it. Lowering her head, she drives forward with all her power and slams me into the wall to my left. With her right hand, she grabs my face just under the nose and slams my head into the wall, once, twice, then a third time.

My vision goes blurry.

Somehow, I'm on the ground and she's on top of me, pinning my arms to the floor. I wrestle my left arm loose and slam my fist into the side of her face. There is blood and sweat covering us both.

She attempts to secure my wrist again but she doesn't notice I've managed to grab my stun gun and flick the switch to turn it on.

"Bold move ... to charge me like that." She pins my right hand with her knee and pulls a large knife from her vest. "But now I'm done with you." She stabs at my chest but I squirm just enough to have the blade pierce my shoulder instead. The pain is white hot. I holler. Her thrust was so powerful, had the blade not been stopped by my collarbone, it might have gone all the way through and pinned me to the floor.

I slide my hand out from underneath her knee and press my fingertips to the wound in her side, applying constant and heavy pressure until she pulls the knife from my shoulder, her mouth agape but emitting no sound. I stop and use the opportunity to slap the knife away. I am starting to feel a little weak from blood loss. The stab wound to my shoulder is bad. This needs to be over.

"Charge this you fuckin' bitch." I lift my head slightly and put the stun gun to the side of her rib cage, letting the voltage do its job. Contrary to popular belief, the current will not pass through her and into me with this kind of close contact stun gun, so I'm safe.

She screams, jolts, then falls off of me to her right.

Just to be sure, I press the stun gun to her leg and hit the button again. Her muscles twitch but she seems unconscious. I sincerely hope she pissed and shit herself.

I let my head rest back. I'm dizzy and lightheaded. If she comes to, I don't know if I will have the strength to fight her off again. I can hardly keep my eyes open. With the wound in her side and the one in my shoulder, it appears we'll both lay here and die together. I would rather this have gone a different way but some part of me is fine with the idea of this outcome. Perhaps it was inevitable, her killing me in this house like she should have twenty years ago, and me killing her now for breaking every rule in the book of assassins.

An image comes to mind, the one from the picture I took from Allister Coal's business office. If I had the energy to smile I would but I'm fading fast. I let my body fully relax as my mind drifts.

39

A decision

One by one, AWT's former leadership staff, including Ollie, Li Xia, Marty, Tisha, Greg, and Nazir, step into the house where Josey and Madame K are on the floor of the living room. Dr. Chardy was not privy to the plan, nor any part of it. He lacked the history to understand or be involved in anyway, and would likely have compromised the plan.

Nazir kneels by both of them and checks their pulses. "They're both alive, barely," he says. He examines Madame K first. "She has a pretty bad wound on her side, bleeding out." He moves on to check Josey. He lifts her head and notes the blood on the back of her head. He spots the pool at her collarbone area and can see the severity of it. "She was stabbed too." He points to Josey's shoulder. "Looks like a good old-fashioned knife fight."

"Wouldn't have expected that," Greg says.

They form a semi-circle around the women.

"Now what do we do?" Ollie asks.

"As far as I'm concerned, we can let them both die," Li Xia says. "She launched shutdown protocol, just like we thought she would. What do we care now?"

"How can you say that?" Ollie snaps. "Josey did nothing to deserve this fate."

"She did nothing to avoid it either, in all honesty," Tisha chimes in.

"That seems a little harsh," Greg says.

"If we're going to do anything, we need to decide quickly," Nazir rises. "They're not going to last much longer."

"I have to say," Li Xia says, "I'm shocked that Josey managed to get this far with Madame K. I guarantee that was no easy task. Obviously, she might pay for it with her life, but still."

"Time's ticking," Marty says. "Let's make a decision here."

"Yeah," Tisha adds. "Anybody could drive by right now. We need to leave."

From the floor, a voice. "Congrat-ulations," Madame K chokes out. She lifts and turns her head ever so slightly to bear witness to who is standing before her. There's a noticeable wheeze in her breathing. "A well-laid ... plan. I expect-ed ... nothing less. I trained ... you all ... well."

The group looks to the face of their former boss but say nothing. Coming into the house, they had no idea what they might find. They waited outside for things to quiet down. When the gunfire ceased and no one emerged after a few minutes, they entered to see what damage had been done. Most of them expected to find Josey dead but hoped for the opposite, and Madame K at least wounded. They had no intention of leaving their old boss alive, regardless. To them, she represented the cure, the disease, and the root cause.

Ollie has a great deal he would like to say to Madame K in this moment but they all agreed beforehand not to speak to her. The plan was to arrive, see how things turned out, and intervene, but only if necessary to ensure Madame K did make it out alive. Josey seems to have accomplished the later part of that on her own. If there was any doubt in Ollie's respect for Josey, it was all but eliminated when they walked through the doorway.

Madame K's head relaxes back down to the floor.

Ollie looks to Li Xia, who offers up a hand gesture to signify passing the decision to him.

"Well," Ollie says, "It's time for a future with all this shit behind us."

There are nods and consensus.

Using a cell phone, Li Xia calls for a cleanup crew, one they arranged outside of AWT.

40

I'm standing still but the world around me is whizzing by, bright streaks of light surrounding me on all sides. I can't see anyone but I hear them, feel them. My mind is slipping away. I try to cry out for help, and in the distance, muffled voices answer. The words, however, are lost on me.

I try hard to focus on the voices. I call to them again. I start to see faces in the flashes of light. Dina manifests before me then disappears. Wayne Leer does the same. I reach out. They're too far to touch and covered in blood. I'm feeling desperate for help, scared. I hear Rosemary's voice telling me to let go, then Emily's voice saying the same. They appear before me too, bloodied and angry, but they fade away as quickly as they had arrived. A bunch of other faces fly by too but with no voices. I recognize them as all the people I have killed in my work for AWT.

From behind me, a man's voice, one I'm happy to hear. Sake Tom, my mentor and friend, and someone whose death I was not responsible for. A most welcome change.

I turn and find him standing, or maybe floating in front of

me. I smile, then turn sad as I realize I might be dead.

"I tried, Tom. I tried but she beat me. It's over and all of this was for nothing."

"This is not the end, Josey," he says. "Not even close."

"But I think I'm dead."

"A part of you has died, yes, but another part of you is being reborn. You're going to close a miserable chapter in your life and write a whole new story, but this time, you'll do it accepting who you are instead of always fighting it. Because of that, everything will be different, better."

A melancholy wave runs over me. I want to cry. "I miss you, Sake Tom."

"And you always will."

"What do I do now?"

"Look in the mirror." He smiles then fades into a wisp of light, leaving me standing in the bathroom of my childhood home.

The room is dimly lit but my tired and teary eyes see a little girl staring back at me from the mirror. Over her shoulder appears a masked woman, only her eyes visible. I turn around and find nothing. Back at the mirror, the woman charges forward and just as she reaches the little girl, the mirror shatters into a thousand little pieces. The noise is deafening. I scream and put my hands in front of my face to shield myself.

"You're okay, honey. You were having a dream, bad one by the sounds of it. But you're safe now." She uses a button somewhere near the foot of the bed to shift me to a position closer to sitting up. She then adjusts my pillows to make it more comfortable.

Confusion and pain. There's a woman I don't know standing beside me. She's wearing pink scrubs. She's short like me, her blonde hair pulled into a high-set ponytail. She's checking a heart monitor next to me and jotting down something on a chart.

I touch my face. The left side is bandaged, as is the top of my head and my shoulder. There are tubes coming from my left arm and my hands are bruised. I suddenly remember Madame K slamming my head into the wall, which explains that and the headache. I also remember the burning sensation of her sliding a blade into my shoulder as we fought. I'm sure I look absolutely fabulous right now, like the victim of an attempted murder.

"Am I going to be okay?" I ask, wondering if attempted murder was the right phrase to be thinking about here.

"You've been knocked out for forty-eight hours. You had a concussion, a lot of scraps and blunt force trauma, but we fixed up that nasty stab wound. A two-hour surgery for that. Tip of a knife broke off in there. But in answer to your question, yes, you are recovering nicely and will likely be okay."

"The other woman. Was there another woman?"

"No, honey. You're the only one here."

"In the whole hospital?"

"There's someone waiting outside in the hallway for you. Let me go get him."

She leaves.

Thirty second later, Ollie walks through the door and comes right to my bedside.

I cover my eyes, ready to cry. I swallow hard after a lump develops in my throat.

Ollie takes my left hand, gently. After I uncover my eyes, he looks to me with a sincerity I've never seen in him. He's genuinely glad to see me.

I want to grill him and I'm sure he must know I have so many questions.

"She's gone, Josey. And so is AWT. Everything is going to be fine."

My lower lip quivers and my eyes well up.

"Just rest and heal up. There are big things ahead for us. A whole new start. When the time is right, I'll sit down and fill you in on all the details."

I start to cry.

Ollie squeezes my hand and just lets me sob for a minute.

When I finally calm down, I wipe away the moisture with my sheet.

He reaches over to the nightstand, grabs the box of tissues, and places it in my lap. "Use these. You're such a dude sometimes."

"Oh, Ollie. You say the sweetest things." We chuckle.

"Can I get you anything?"

"Honestly, I'm dying ... oh sorry, that's a poor choice of words, I would love a cup of coffee with cream and the biggest cheeseburger you can find. Vengeance and mayhem sure work up an appetite."

"I'll see what I can do on the coffee and food."

He releases my hand and leaves.

Looking around the room, I can now see that I'm in the same facility where Vick spent months recovering from his spinal injury. This place is intricately linked to AWT, so I'm a bit confused as to how we can be here. This is just one of a thousand questions I have, but I'm tired and can't really get my head to coalesce around most of them.

The important thing is that I'm alive and Madame K is dead. How the hell that came to be is lost on me. My last memory is of lying on the floor at my childhood home, staring up at the peeling and water-stained ceiling. I was certain I was about to die.

I put my hand to my face. There's a build-up of emotions trickling through me. I start sobbing. Here we go again. It's quiet and gentle at first. After fifteen seconds, it goes from murmur, to tremor, to full-on city destroying seismic event. It feels like I've released a lifetime worth of tension and angst. I'm loud enough that the nurse comes running into the room to check on me.

I try to calm down, wiping the tears from my face with my left hand. I grab the tissues and use several to dab my eyes and blow my nose.

Running to my bedside, the nurse asks, "Are you okay?"

Nasally, I answer, "I'm fine." I take a breath through my

mouth, as my sinuses are now clogged up. "Just a lot of shit built up that apparently needed to come out all at once ... again"

"I understand. Is Ollie coming back?"

"Yeah." I blow my nose again. "He went to get me a burger, and hopefully a decent cup of coffee."

"Well, be careful not to get too worked up. You got staples in your shoulder. We don't want to bust one."

I glance over to my shoulder. "I'm guessing that would hurt like a son of bitch?"

She grins and nods vigorously. "I'll come check on you in a bit. Hopefully, Ollie will be back soon with food. You need to eat."

"Okay."

She leaves the room.

I throw the tissues into a little trashcan in front of the bedside table and settle back into bed.

My mind floods with ideas, possibilities, emotions, and people. If I could visit myself during the time right before I joined AWT, what would I say? Run away because it's not worth it? It's about to get real fucked up, but at least you'll know the truth?

I never wondered much about what happened to my parents. I was too young to remember them. I couldn't imagine a nefarious situation revolving around their deaths or how I came to be with Rosemary. Had I never joined AWT, I wouldn't know any of this. I'm glad I do, but I don't know that I'm better off for it.

There was always a slight itch in my head that pondered their possible fate, and sure, that's gone, but now it's simply been replaced with different questions. What would my life be like had they never been killed? If Madame K had indeed gone through with her plan to train me as assassin from a young age, what would my life have been like?

The only respite I have is knowing that Madame K's responsibility in all this has been paid in full. Where that leaves me, I don't know. I have a lot of soul-searching to do in the coming months. Part of this process has been discovering who I am, deep, deep down. All I know is that Daniel, Annie, and Kiki Jones died in that house, and what's left is me, Josey Baldwin, a living, breathing contradiction.

A lover *and* a fighter.

A good person *and* a killer.

Epilogue

Six months after the death of Madame K

My shoulder is finally healed up but it will never be one hundred percent right again. Thankfully, I still have full range of motion, it just aches when it rains, aches when I use it too much, aches when it's cold. Let's just say, I'll be buying jumbo-sized bottles of ibuprofen for the rest of my life.

Right now, I'm on a mission. I'm doing recon from inside a white van with the name of a fake plumbing company on the outside of it. My future target is in a building just up the block. At some point, he's going to leave and I'll have to follow. Until then, I will sit here, sipping on coffee and munching on beef jerky. So far, it's been almost two hours of just watching and waiting.

AWT, of course, is gone. I'm part of a new consortium led by Ollie. It's a smaller organization, with everyone involved an equal partner. There is no Kill Academy and no kill teams. We operate with no dummy corporation to hide behind and no fixed base of operations. Instead, we use foreign accounts and other methods for the money part, and a more mobile and fluid sense of home, although, we are beginning to acquire a few safehouse locations around the country to use when needed.

Greg and Li Xia retired from the trade, which was no surprise to anyone. I miss their passion but we're doing fine. Vick now serves as our weapons expert and Nazir is spearheading our fitness and training, in addition to his guidance in recon. Amatto and I handle Point on all missions, but we do have our eyes on a few prospects to bring in. Thankfully, both Marty and Tisha stuck around too, which makes everyone's jobs easier.

Dr. Chardy is also no longer with us. We worked with him

for a time but it didn't take long for him to start creeping us out. He had a real Hannibal Lecter vibe going, so we bounced his ass out of here. We now have Dr. Roslyn Davies, and she's working out well in the role of team counselor. We tossed around the idea of not having someone in that position, but after a long, hard look into the benefits we derived from Dina's work, we unanimously decided it would be better if we did. Plus, we're all a bunch of animals and she's the only one around here that will look at every situation logically and without all the angst and bitterness that most of us carry.

While I healed and rehabbed my shoulder over a few months, I took all that time to evaluate the last few years, where I've been and where I'm going. As part of the process, I decided there were lines as an assassin I would not cross. I won't kill children, ever, and I won't accept any contract where the target is not a verifiably rotten human being. No taking out corporate whistleblowers, or simple adulterers, or none of that *'my ex-wife is a bitch and I just want her dead'* bullshit. The rest of the consortium agreed and that is how we operate now.

It took me a long time to figure out who I am, but once I did and I accepted it, life and my state of mind have been more at peace. I live on the wrong side of the tracks, in the shadows, and I'm a killer, for better or for worse. And I'm damn good at it. Accepting that simple truth has been my path to being content. It means I can't have meaningful and personal relationships with people outside of my dark bubble. It means I will always have to look over my shoulder wherever I go. It also means I'm dangerous and no one to be trifled with.

So, if you're a person who's into some bad shit, watch your ass. If the money is right, I might just show up in your bedroom and blow your fuckin' head off.

ABOUT THE AUTHOR

Richard's sixth major release, Kill Alone, the conclusion of the Kill Series, continues the story of Josey Baldwin as she faces the truth of her past on her way to discovering who she really is. His previous works include Kill Team – Kill Series Book Two (2018), Kill Academy - Kill Series Book One (2017), RejectGuy99 (2015), A Room Full of Keys (2013), & Neither Snow, Nor Rain, Nor Zombie Infection (2012).

He currently makes his home in Central Illinois with his wife, Amy, and their Cavachon, Padraig. Reading, writing, playing videogames, watching independent films, and DIY projects are among his favorite pastimes.

Richard communicates best through movie lines and song lyrics, and is often lost in the pop-language of past generations. For example, he would like to bring back the terms knockin' boots & breeches.

RICHARD A. POWELL II